Fake Plastic Girl

Fake Plastic Girl

Zara Lisbon

HENRY HOLT AND COMPANY

NEW YORK

To my grandmothers,
Ellie and Doreen

Henry Holt and Company, *Publishers since 1866*
Henry Holt® is a registered trademark of Macmillan Publishing Group, LLC
175 Fifth Avenue, New York, New York 10010 • fiercereads.com
Copyright © 2019 by Spilled Ink, Inc.

Library of Congress Control Number: 2018945020

ISBN 978-1-250-15629-7

Our books may be purchased in bulk for promotional, educational, or business
use. Please contact your local bookseller or the Macmillan Corporate and
Premium Sales Department at (800) 221-7945 ext. 5442 or by email at
MacmillanSpecialMarkets@macmillan.com.

First edition, 2019 / Designed by Liz Dresner

Printed in the United States of America

10 9 8 7 6 5 4 3 2 1

I'm an angel compared to some of my friends.

—Lindsay Lohan

Growing up I was always prone to obsession, partly because of the way I am, but partly because after feeling so lonely for such a long time, when I found someone or something that I liked, I felt helplessly drawn to it.

—Lana Del Rey

CHAPTER 1

THE BODY
IN THE CANAL

*E*va-Kate Kelly.

Is this story really about a person with three first names? Could anything be more tedious than a person with three first names? I know you, I can imagine you rolling your eyes thinking you're too good for a girl with three first names, let alone an entire story about a girl with three first names, but the truth is most likely that no matter who you are and no matter how hard you're capable of rolling your eyes, Eva-Kate Kelly would love that you think you're too good for her and her three first names, she would revel in the few short moments it took her to prove you wrong, she would chew you up and she would spit you out, she would impale you with the fire-green lasers that were her eyes, stare into you and then through you, so that you'd wonder if you ever existed at all. It would take you months to recover and you'd never really be the same again. That was the Eva-Kate I first came to know, anyway.

✻ ✻ ✻

They found her body floating in the canal. Nothing would ever be the same after that. I mean, how could it be, right? One day she's alive and thriving and the next she's purple and spongy, lying facedown in mossy water. Gone. The headlines ran like ticker tape:

HOLLYWOOD STARLET
DROWNS IN VENICE CANAL

SEVENTEEN-YEAR-OLD STAR OF
"JENNIE AND JENNY" FOUND DEAD

EVA-KATE KELLY STABBED TO DEATH

THE DEATH OF EVA-KATE KELLY—A GAME
TAKEN TOO FAR OR MURDER IN COLD BLOOD?

The last one I hated most. What happened to Eva-Kate wasn't a game taken too far and it wasn't murder. It was something else entirely.

CHAPTER 2

DANGEROUS, DEVIOUS, DEVIANT

*I*n eighth grade, Ms. Norris told me I had a gift as a writer. She wasn't the first person to say so, actually. In fifth grade, Beachwood Elementary published a short story I'd written about one half of a best friend necklace lost at the beach—"The Sand Locket"—in their monthly paper. In second grade, I won first place at the district poetry contest. My poem was a set of couplets expressing concern that one day technology could become so advanced we'd no longer have a reason to leave our homes. It was sappy, clichéd, and naive in a charmless way, but as far as the judges were concerned, it was the best four rhyming lines a seven-year-old had ever written.

So Ms. Norris wasn't the first person to appreciate my writing, but she was the first person to suggest one day it could make me famous. The suggestion was vague and probably part of some contract teachers sign agreeing to encourage X number of kids per year to aim for the moon/ dream as if they'll live forever and all that, but I latched onto it. All I had to do, she said, was find the right story to tell.

Never in a million years did I expect to have such a story walk into my life and all but beg to be written down. And never in a million years did I believe I'd have an audience all but beg to hear my side of things. Yet, here we are.

A lot of what you've heard out there about what happened that summer is fake news. They tell you that I was a girl obsessed, that I was dangerous, devious, deviant. They tell you about the psychiatric hospital like it was an asylum for the criminally insane, about the knife and the blood and my fingerprints. All of it to sell magazines, none of it true. I have to at least try to set the record straight.

CHAPTER 3

FEARLESS

*T*he story starts with Chasen's.

Chasen's, as you may know, was a Beverly Hills restaurant for Hollywood's elite. But as you almost *certainly* know, it was also the title of a 2009 rom com about some fictional events leading to the restaurant's nonfictional closing back in 1995. The movie starred Rachel Ames, who was, at the time, the highest-paid actress in Hollywood. Incidentally, she was also my mom's patient.

As a therapist, my mom—Nancy Childs, PhD—was strict about never revealing the identities of her patients, and it's really not her fault that I found out. Or that I'm telling you about it now. But I was eight and it was a Saturday and we had just gotten in line at Ben & Jerry's when she received an emergency patient call. Rachel

Ames was in crisis and needed her on set ASAP. It's not like my mom was going to leave me alone in Ben & Jerry's, so what choice did she really have?

That's how I ended up on the set of *Chasen's*, eight years old and dressed head to toe in glittery snowflakes—sans ice cream—from Gap's winter catalog.

"Dr. Childs, Jesus Christ." Rachel Ames was trembling as we approached her standing outside a silver Star Waggon, her own name scrawled on the door in Sharpie. She wore a gold-beaded shawl over her bony arms and Tom Ford sunglasses so big they eclipsed her entire eye sockets, even the top part of her dramatically angular cheekbones. Tough but friendly-looking men stood five feet from her on both sides, arms crossed, pretending to be more machine than human.

"What happened, Rachel?" my mom asked sweetly, calm as a light breeze with her seashell-pink cardigan buttoned up all the way. Suddenly overtaken by a spell of shyness, I hid behind her linen pencil skirt and pinched nervously at the fabric.

"Benji's cheating on me," Rachel Ames said, her upper lip quivering. "He's been cheating on me. This whole time." That was Benji Laramore, her A-list actor husband of three years. Rumor had it their agents had originally set them up on a date as a publicity stunt, but surprisingly to all involved, it ended up being love at first sight.

"Well, okay now." My mom remained unruffled, not even vaguely fazed. "What makes you think—"

"No, no." Rachel laughed bitterly. "You don't understand. This isn't a theory. This is fact. And how do I find out?" She held up a tattered copy of *Us Weekly* and shoved the cover page into my mom's face. I craned my neck and peered upward to read the headline: "Benji Laramore Leaves Rachel Ames for Dominique Le Bon." Beneath it, a paparazzi shot of Benji and Dominique laughing gleefully on a park bench in Paris.

Dominique Le Bon. Third- or fourth-highest-paid actress in Hollywood that year, but arguably the single most beautiful woman in the world. While Rachel Ames was pretty, an American golden girl—the good girl, no doubt—Dominique Le Bon's beauty was extraterrestrial. Smoky cat eyes and luscious lips perpetually pouting in seductive discontent, a stomach so flat and breasts so round it would hardly be surprising to learn she wasn't even human at all. And yet, she maintained that she'd never had any work done. And rumor had it she was telling the truth.

"Oh dear." My mom took the magazine from Rachel's hands and studied the cover.

"That's right," Rachel breathed, incredulous. "Not just cheating, but in love. Divorcing me. And of course *she* gave *Us Weekly* the whole story, *he'd* never have the balls. I thought he'd at least have the balls to tell *me* himself, but I guess I was wrong. Either he doesn't have the balls or he plain old doesn't have respect for me." A tear slid down beneath one Tom Ford lens and she dabbed at it with her shawl, then looked at me and froze, as if only just then realizing I was there.

"I'm sorry, Dr. Childs, I didn't mean to say *balls* in front of your daughter."

"It's not a problem, Rachel. This is a uniquely painful situation."

"Can she wait out here while we go talk inside?" She gestured to the trailer door. "I'm gonna say a lot more ugly words and I don't want her to hear me talk like that."

"Don't worry." My mom patted her bulky leather handbag. "I have an iPod and noise-canceling headphones. She won't hear a thing."

"Actually, I'd prefer it if she stayed out here anyway. I need a cigarette and I absolutely can't have her seeing me smoke. She'd tell all her friends, and I really don't want kids thinking of me like this. I'm supposed to be this strong female role model and look at me! This is humiliating."

I thought it was a strange thing for her to say, that she didn't want me to see her smoke, because now I knew she smoked and would probably tell my friends anyway. I definitely would, I decided, because she'd hurt my feelings assuming that I couldn't keep a secret.

"Hey, no." My mom rested her arm lightly on Rachel's

arm. "You don't have to explain yourself. Justine will stay right here." She reached into her bag and handed me the iPod and noise-canceling headphones, saying, "This won't take long, sweetie. And we'll go back to Ben & Jerry's right after. I owe you an ice cream, okay?"

Then I was standing alone holding an iPod in one hand and noise-canceling headphones in the other, not sure what to do next because nothing on the iPod was half as interesting as what I knew was going on behind that trailer door. I sat down on the steps and tried to hear what they were saying, but every word was muffled and garbled by the aluminum walls between us. Cigarette smoke wafted out through the mesh-screen windows.

I don't think I would have particularly cared about what it looked like inside a movie star's trailer if it weren't for me not being allowed in one. I hated being on the outside, like I hadn't earned my way in, like maybe I never would. On my mom's 2002 iPod I listened to *Fearless* by Taylor Swift, the entire album, and with my eyes closed I could hear just how fearless this girl really was. She poured her awkward teenage heart into each lyric and didn't care what people thought of it, or, even more fearlessly, she *did* care but wrote it down and sang it out anyway. I admired the hell out of that. In fifth grade, when I was asked to read "The Sand Locket" out loud for my class, I refused. Just the idea of standing up in front of thirty other students made my legs shake so wildly I knew I wouldn't make it to the podium, let alone manage to force my mouth open once I got up there. But back at home that night, I'd cried—no, sobbed—because I'd *wanted* to read my story. I just couldn't. I wasn't fearless. And I worried that I never would be.

As the album played through, I thought about how in 2007 she'd played her first song (and first hit), "Tim McGraw," in front of Tim McGraw himself at the Country Music Awards. She'd strolled right up to where he sat in the audience and serenaded him on live TV, not a hint of insecurity on her ceramic face, not even the slightest tremor in her voice. Even at seventeen she knew with every inch of herself that she deserved to be there; she knew she'd earned her way in. I thought, if she were me right now, she'd knock down the trailer door and declare injustice on the whole thing, or she'd run away and make them rue the day they locked her out. But I did neither. I wasn't fearless.

It was two hours later before my mom finally came out, pulling the door closed quickly behind her, smelling strongly of smoke and perfume. The sun was down and I was shivering, the title track playing for the tenth or eleventh time, Taylor singing: *You take my hand and drag me headfirst, fearless.*

"More Taylor Swift?" My mom wrinkled her nose, snatching the iPod from my hand. "Of all the real music I have on there, you choose *Taylor Swift?*"

Yes, I wanted to say, *and what do you know about real music? You think because she's new and maybe a little naive and a seventeen-year-old hopeless romantic that her music isn't real? Did you know she writes it all herself? Did you know she doesn't care whether you think her music is real or not? Did you know if I could I'd be her right now instead of me and tell you that I'm cold and tired and hungry and that you hurt my feelings leaving me out here for so long and that you owe me an ice cream?*

But instead I said, "Yes. She's fearless."

"Great," my mom said. "Now I've heard everything."

I sat quietly in the back seat as she drove us home, and as we passed Ben & Jerry's I said nothing, my nose pressed up against the car window, practically lusting after the pink neon ice cream cone glowing in the dark. I wanted the ice cream, yes, but there was something I wanted more now: to get on the inside, and to be fearless when I got there.

CHAPTER 4

FAME AND ANONYMITY

*J*ump to the last day of tenth grade, probably one of the most important days of my life. I was sixteen and still nursing a bruised ego about the night spent outside Rachel Ames's trailer. Though I tried not to, I still believed that I'd been left out in the cold because I wasn't important. If I'd been an important person, Rachel Ames would have wanted me in there with her. She would have placed a cigarette in my tiny eight-year-old hand and said, "Okay, Justine, tell me what *you* think." Do you see what my mind can do to itself sometimes?

And it wasn't just Rachel Ames and it wasn't just my mom. Growing up in Los Angeles with two parents who rubbed elbows with celebrities—Mom adored it, Dad resented it—put me in an odd *Twilight Zone*–style limbo between two different worlds: the world of fame and the world of anonymity. Normally, if you're rich and famous, you don't ever have to stand in the rain waiting for the bus with a drenched gaggle of teenagers and local schizophrenics who have wandered up Pico Boulevard from the beach, and normally, if you are not rich and famous, you don't get to stand with your nose pressed up against the glass box in which these enigmatic creatures live. Unless you're me. I was a non-famous, an anonymous, with front-row seats to the most in-demand show of the century, and never to be allowed onstage. It was fucking surreal.

You want examples? No problem. Here's a list, in no particular order, of ten times I was a Hollywood outsider on the Hollywood inside.

1. I'm nine years old, taking after-school classes at Brentwood Art Academy. My dad has paid the academy in paintings, not money. Suri Cruise is in my class. She's four years old but dressed to kill in her multi-patterned sundresses and oversized satin hair bows. I'm jealous of her for everything she is and has, my friends at school are jealous of me just because I know her. I hate being jealous of a four-year-old. Katie and Tom pick her up at the end of each day

in Tom's Bugatti Veyron. My mom wants to know how short he looks in person. I don't know, I say, he's taller than me.

2. I'm twelve years old and losing friends because I'm the only one developing breasts. My mom meets Joni Mitchell at a party and the two hit it off, end up deep in conversation back at her Bel Air mansion. That year Joni Mitchell calls to wish me a happy birthday and invites me to her next show. News of this makes me highly popular for about a week, before the other kids realize they don't really know who Joni Mitchell even is, and then forget entirely.

3. I'm six years old and obsessed with Mary-Kate and Ashley Olsen. Our next-door neighbor is their makeup artist and she agrees to take me to a photo shoot. The shoot is supposed to be set in London, but actually takes place on a set in LA that looks like London. Mary-Kate and Ashley introduce themselves as Mary-Kate and Ashley. They're sweet and friendly as angels. They smell like daisies and mint and I'm too shy to say anything. They're very busy,

but if I want I can stay and watch them get their makeup done. So I do.

4. I'm ten years old and Rachel Bilson's cousin starts going to my mom for therapy. Rachel Bilson's cousin has a bunch of Rachel Bilson's clothes that Rachel Bilson doesn't want anymore. She's a size zero in everything, and at ten years old, so am I. For the next two years I wear designer label outfits rejected by Rachel Bilson.

5. I'm eight years old and Arnold Schwarzenegger's son is on my softball team. He's at all the games. I'm the only one who doesn't give a fuck.

6. I'm eleven years old and Julia Roberts moves into a house down the street. She hires me to water her garden and pays me fifty dollars every time. Emma Roberts watches me from the porch. One day she gives me her Dolce & Gabbana headband. I treasure it forever.

7. I'm thirteen years old and my mom is working with someone on the cast of *Mad Men*,

though she won't tell me who. She gets us invited to the screening of the finale at the Ace Hotel downtown. At the rooftop after-party, she gets lost in a conversation with John Slattery. I wander away and sit alone by the Jacuzzi with the *Mad Men* logo projected onto the water. A man who says he's a producer sits next to me and holds out a drink. He says it's called an old-fashioned and puts his hand on my thigh. Immediately, I hate him for it. I stand up abruptly, accidentally knocking the drink out of his hand and into the Jacuzzi. He's mad, quietly calls me a cunt. I hurry away and hide in the hallway, crying. Jon Hamm finds me there and takes pity, helps me find my mom.

8. I'm seven years old and my babysitter is also Willow Smith's babysitter. We're invited to a Labor Day BBQ with the Smiths. I don't remember being there, but you can bet my mom saved the pictures.

9. I'm fourteen years old and a friend of a friend is dating Reese Witherspoon's daughter. We're at the mall and Reese picks

us up in her Range Rover. I have her drop me off down the block so nobody will see the tiny house I live in.

10. I'm fifteen years old and it's summer and I get a job at a ritzy horse-riding camp in Malibu where Taylor Swift keeps a horse. Everything is "Taylor this" and "Taylor that." She's all they can talk about. It drives me crazy.

Get the idea? Great.

Okay, so, back to the last day of tenth grade.

Sorry to skip ahead so abruptly like that; I know I'm not the most graceful of storytellers. Of course I'd like to write this novel as seamlessly as the greats are able to, jumping elegantly across time periods and tenses, making elaborate choices of style and structure, holding the plot tightly by its reins. But this is the first book I've ever written, and so I will by no means have the plot by its reins. This plot won't even have reins. It will have seams, and you will see them.

But anyway, it was the last day of tenth grade and we were sitting on The Hill—Maddie, Abbie, Riley, and me—eating lunch. We weren't actually eating lunch (we ate lunch after school at Cafe 50's), but it was lunch break and everyone was dispersed across campus in their designated lunch-eating territories. The Hill was ours. It was prime real estate—we got to look down on the Hot Topic Punks who sat on the brick steps and the school-spirited popular kids who gathered around blue picnic benches in the science quad—but the real estate was worth nothing in my mind, because if we were actually cool we'd be "eating lunch" off campus, where the non-school-spirited popular kids went. The kids with parents laid-back enough to sign off-campus permission slips, and the kids deviously capable enough to forge their parents' signatures. My parents would have signed the slip, but what good would it do me if all my friends were stuck on the wrong side of the fence? The sad thing is, in their minds they weren't stuck; they wanted to stay on campus during lunch. Or so they said. Stockholm syndrome, IMHO.

"Should we leave?" I asked the group, tiredly gazing at the front gate, which was currently unguarded by the normal glorified janitors who stood there like medieval goblins and barked at anyone trying to leave without an off-campus pass.

"We can't," Riley said, clearly confused by my suggestion. "We have two more classes left." Riley I'd known since fifth grade. We saw everything eye to eye, once upon a time. She was a redhead with unruly freckles and what people like to call a "free spirit." Out of the two of our spirits, hers had always been the freer one, anyone would have told you that. But as tenth grade came to a close I felt that despite its freedom, her spirit lacked imagination. Her idea of an adventure was taking the bus east on Wilshire to an all-hours café that permitted indoor smoking, playing board games with strangers until four in the morning.

"Yeah, but how much could we possibly miss? I mean, *really*. It's literally the last day, you know they're just gonna put on some Civil War documentary and call it a lesson."

"My fifth period is marine biology," said Abbie. "Mr. Cameron isn't going to be putting on any Civil War documentary." Of everyone in our group, Abbie was my least favorite. She was the kind of girl who denied getting her eyebrows shaped despite their obvious, unnatural perfection, the kind of girl who loved Taylor Swift but pretended not to.

"Okay, even better," I tried. "He'll probably put on, like, what? *Finding Nemo*?"

Riley giggled.

"If you're caught ditching class it goes on your permanent record," Maddie reminded us. "Colleges can see it." She took a chewed-up piece of Winterfresh gum from her mouth, stuck it into a silver wrapper, and rolled it into a tight ball. Then, with French-tipped nails, she unwrapped two new sticks. She was a chain gum-chewer, she didn't go anywhere without at least two packs of Winterfresh.

And she always chewed two sticks at a time; if she ended a pack with only one stick left, she'd save it in her wallet for when she had a second piece to go with it. I wondered if the wet, smacking sound was as loud in her head as it was to the rest of us.

"What college do you think is going to possibly care that in tenth grade you skipped the second half of the last day of school?" I asked.

"Harvard will," said Maddie. "They have over thirty thousand straight-A students competing to get in, they look at every tiny detail to weed people out."

"Oh please." Abbie rolled her eyes. "You've been unqualified for Harvard since you failed Intro to Art History."

"You wish." Maddie threw her wrapped piece of chewed Winterfresh at Abbie. "Then I'd have to stay here and go to whatever bullshit state school you'll end up at."

"I'm not going to a state school," Abbie pouted. She tended to be able to dish it out but never take it. "I got a 1330 on my PSATs."

"Right, well, see, I got a 1495." Maddie chewed triumphantly.

"Stop!" I was so bored I wanted to literally crawl out of my skin. "Do we really have to be worrying about college right now? It's summer. And we won't be applying to schools for like two years."

"Actually," Maddie began, "it's really more like one ye—"

"Fuck college," Riley interrupted.

"Here we go." Abbie took out a compact mirror, as if looking at her reflection would block out whatever Riley had to say.

"It's a scam," Riley went on. "You pay a hundred grand to some stuffy institution just so you can put it on a résumé in hope of getting hired to work somewhere corporate from nine to five until you die? And if you don't have the hundred grand—and really, who does?—then you have to borrow it and end up being in debt to the government for literally the rest of your life. So, no thanks." She threw her hands up in surrender. "Not me."

"So you got a better plan, genius?" Maddie asked.

"Please don't encourage her like that," Abbie pleaded. "If I have to hear her tell it one more time I'll shoot myself."

"Tell what?" I asked.

"Her plan for after high school," Abbie told us.

"I've never heard it," I said, a little hurt. Though not too hurt, because I'd never told Riley my plans either. I didn't think she could handle them.

"Me either," said Maddie, seemingly pleased with the discomfort she was causing.

"I'm gonna move to upstate New York," Riley said proudly, "and wait tables at a diner."

"That's . . . *that's* it?" asked Maddie. "You want to be a waitress? You can do that *here*, you know, you don't have to be in the middle of nowhere."

"Yeah, but I want to be in the middle of nowhere," Riley said wistfully. "I want to walk barefoot through tall grasses and marry a local musician and have ten babies."

"I don't understand." Maddie furrowed her brow. She was stumped.

"It's just her way of making herself feel like she's different than everyone else," Abbie explained. "She wants you to think she's above your capitalist desires and conformist ideals." As if she were above Riley's trying to be above everyone else.

"Sure, you could see it like that." Riley shrugged. "Doesn't really matter to me. All I care about is that I'll be the one enjoying life while y'all are commuting to a job you hate." She turned to me then. "Justine, you get it, don't you?"

I hated when she said *y'all* like she was some kind of Southern belle, when really she'd never been outside Los Angeles. And I hated that to her the entire world was laid out in black and white.

"I get it," I said, mostly because between the two of them my loyalty stood with Riley. "Everyone has their own path. If that's what you want to do, you should do it."

The truth was I thought Riley's vision for the future sounded just as flat and dry as the future all our parents wanted us to have with the undergraduate degree and the six-figure income and the stability. To me, Riley's vision was just another version of dreaming small.

"Hey." We looked up to see Michael Cross standing

over us with Autumn Mercer and Christa Rooney. They were juniors, a year older than we were, and represented the elite of the non-school-spirited popular kids. In other words, they were gorgeous and well-dressed in high-end vintage clothing and acted like they absolutely did not give a fuck what you or anyone else thought of them. They were only talking to us because I had fourth-period California Literature with Michael, and was the one sophomore in the class. Maddie and Abbie gawked; Riley pretended to get a text.

"Oh, hey," I said, squinting into the sun, not sure if I should stand to greet them. "What's up?"

"We're just heading down to the bowling alley. I saw you sitting here so I thought I'd come see if you wanted to join us for some milkshakes and chill."

Michael had brownish-red hair and uniquely blessed bone structure. Girls swooned over him and anxiously fretted over the question of his sexual orientation. But I didn't care about any of that, I just thought he was so cool with his Doc Martens and pinstriped jeans and clear-framed glasses. He readjusted the strap of his messenger bag and waited for my answer.

"Like, *all of us*?" Maddie blurted.

"No, thanks." Riley looked up from her phone long enough to intervene. "We have plans."

"Oh . . . okay, then." Michael looked almost disappointed. Autumn and Christa looked like they couldn't possibly have cared less. "Have a good summer, Justine."

"Yeah . . . you too," I stammered as he waved goodbye. "I . . . I'll see you in September."

"So, what"—Riley looked back down at her phone— "are you in love with him all of a sudden?"

"What the fuck was that, Riley?" I glared at her.

"Come on, JuJu, you didn't actually want to go hang with them, did you?"

"You *know* I did."

"Oh well," she sighed. "I'd say I'm sorry, but it's just for your own good."

"My own *good*? What the hell do you—you don't get to decide what's—no, you know what? Forget it." I stood up just as the bell rang and brushed the twigs off my jeans.

"Justine, where are you going?" Abbie called out after me, but I didn't really have an answer for her, so I just kept walking.

✱ ✱ ✱

I threw my backpack over the fence behind the English building and climbed after it. Then I was free.

Looking over my shoulder every few feet, I power walked down Pico Boulevard to the corner of Fourth Street, paranoid that a gate guard might see me. I stood on the corner, nervously waiting for the light to change, thrilling fear in the form of a hot shiver racing up my spine, certain that any second someone would sneak up from behind and catch me in the act of trying to have a life, God forbid.

"Finally," I exhaled as the light changed. "Thank God."

I was partially surprised at myself for making it this far, for getting away with it. Once I got to the other side, the nerves melted away and I stood up straight, confident with the knowledge that I was officially in the clear. I took a deep breath and forced myself to keep walking until I got to the bowling alley.

Hey, guys, just thought I'd take you up on that milk-shake and chill. Was that what I'd say? I mulled it over; I moved my mouth silently along the words. No, I decided, don't try so hard.

'Sup? No, too relaxed.

Hey, Michael, thanks for the invite, sorry about Riley, she doesn't know what she's talking about. Too bitchy.

Hey, y'all, how are the milkshakes? Too Riley-y.

Hey, losers, move over. Too edgy.

You know, some say my milkshake brings all the boys to the bowling alley. No way.

What's crackin', fam squad? Too stoned.

"Get over yourself, Justine," I said under my breath. "Just go inside, don't be an idiot."

I walked through the automatic doors and into the glow-in-the-dark-splattered bowling alley, "Any Way You Want It" by Journey raging at full volume. *Okay, so*, I asked myself, glancing around in the dark, *if you were a pack of too-cool-for-school juniors, where would you be?* To my right, a neon sign read BOWLING DINER. FRIES, BURGERS, MILKSHAKES. Beneath the sign was a door with a small window. Far too self-conscious to just stroll on in, I stood on my toes and peered through the glass.

Indeed, there they were, Michael and Autumn and Christa. I had found them. But they weren't just drinking milkshakes and they weren't just chilling. Michael and Autumn sat next to each other in the brown vinyl booth, locked in a passionate kiss, her legs lying over his lap, his hand making its way under her shirt.

OhmyGod. I turned away as fast as I could and darted back out into the blinding sunlight. How could they do that in public? I wondered. And with Christa staring right at them? They'd looked like they were trying to eat each other alive, like somebody should have intervened.

Well, I naively thought, *I guess that ends the mystery of his sexual orientation.*

I didn't know why, but as I stood there with my heart pounding and the new summer sun beating down on my back, I felt let down, even betrayed. I knew I shouldn't—he liked girls, this was good news for all of us!—but something about what I'd seen left me unpleasantly mystified, even alienated, like a kid accidentally walking in on their parents during sex. A familiar weight descended on my chest, the weight of frustration I felt whenever I sensed that I was being shut out of something desirable. Sex, like celebrity, was a world I got to look in on, but was ultimately excluded from. That's how I'd become fixated, that's how I'd become addicted to the dream.

CHAPTER 5

FEMME FATALE

I took the bus home and when I got there, my mom had just finished up with a patient in her office, which once was a guesthouse, in our backyard. She came into the house holding a leather-bound notebook and sighed deeply when she saw me. She looked skinnier than usual in a beige linen pantsuit with her dyed off-blond hair in a short, Hillary Clinton–style cut, exposing the dramatic line of her collarbones. I looked around the living room and noticed how much had gone missing since earlier that morning. The coffee table was gone; so were the bookshelf and my dad's CD collection spread out across three towers. His liquor cabinet was now half-empty.

"Are you supposed to be home yet?" she said nervously, checking her wristwatch. "Is everything okay?"

"They let us out early," I said. "It was the last day of school. Is everything okay with *you*?"

"Oh, right. That's right. Honey, we have to talk," she said, taking a seat on the living room couch.

I knew what this was about; I'd been expecting it for at least five years.

I find this next part of the story to be extremely boring, the only unremarkable piece of the puzzle, so forgive me for rushing through it. Believe me when I say it's for the best, and that you're honestly not missing out on anything.

"You're getting a divorce," I said calmly, standing across from her, holding on to the straps of my turquoise JanSport backpack. "That's it, right?"

"Well, yes," she stuttered. "How'd you know that?"

"Call it intuition." I shrugged, trying to think of something else so I didn't have to think about the millions of ways my life was going to be different from now on. Maybe it didn't have to be different, I thought, or maybe it could be different in all the right ways.

"Do you want to talk about it? I know this can be—"

"I'm fine. But thank you," I interrupted, shutting the door on the conversation and then the literal one to my room, before the awkwardness had a chance to grow and fester into real emotion.

It turns out my dad had already started moving his stuff into a town house in the Valley, where he'd be living with a woman I'd never met or heard of before. And my mom already had a monthlong vacation all planned out, an abbreviated *Eat Pray Love*, something she swore she'd been dying to do way before Elizabeth Gilbert made it popular.

They arranged for me to stay with Aunt Jillian, my mom's sister, who lived with a golden retriever named Kellen in Westwood. Her condo was on the nineteenth floor of one of those towering high-rises on Wilshire and decorated with a disordered display of antiques that she picked up weekly from the Fairfax flea market. The glass cat figurines and collection of rusted, dusty scales from the early 1990s were my favorites.

I liked Aunt Jillian, I really did—her excessive emerald eye shadow, her big pearl earrings, her veneers—but I'd kill myself before spending an entire month with her. So when I found her bottles of Percocet hidden underneath a floor tile in the bathroom, we made a deal: I wouldn't tell my mom about her pill problem and she wouldn't tell my mom I was staying by myself in our empty waterfront house until further notice.

✳ ✳ ✳

That was easy enough, I thought on my first night alone, climbing into bed with my clothes still on. *By the time my mom gets home, by the time school starts again, the Justine everyone knew will be dead.* I vowed then to spin myself into the sophisticated femme fatale I'd longed to be, to spend the summer collecting experiences like poker chips in a towering stack, to become so worldly and self-assured that when school started in the fall, nobody would recognize me. If only I knew where to begin.

CHAPTER 6

LARGER THAN LIFE

*T*he first time I saw her in person she was nothing more than a paper cutout of a girl, a silhouette, still nameless, with slender arms and ripened hips, hair so long and thick it poured like milk over her bony shoulders.

It was one week after my parents had left me, and I was sitting on the porch swing with Princess Leia, our two-year-old labradoodle, on my lap. I had an open tube of raw cookie dough sitting next to me and my 2010 MacBook Pro open on the outdoor coffee table so I could click through I Know What You Did Last Night. For those of you who don't know, IKWYDLN was an online photo gallery of LA's most exclusive parties featuring mostly celebrities (A-list through D-list) and hipster models and anonymous underage girls getting wasted in decadent settings, often with cigarettes dangling from their lips and always tons of flash. Don't bother looking it up, though; the site got taken down after everything that happened.

But in the website's heyday, photographs were organized by night, and each night got a title, word combinations I never understood like "Nylon Let's Go" or "Spooky Youth Twelve." I'd realize later those combinations were intentionally nonsensical so it would appear esoteric, vaguely poetic, a code you'd certainly be able to decipher if only you weren't so out of touch, so out of tune. The truth is, I realize now, those word combinations didn't mean anything at all, not to Spencer Sawyer (famed photographer and curator of the site) or to anyone. The whole thing was designed to make you feel like you'd never be cool enough to "get it." You'd click on one and be taken to a page of about fifty photos that would guide you in time from the beginning of the party when everyone is in makeup and heels, to the very end when the makeup is smudged and the heels are off and the cups are empty and the sun is rising outside and people are sitting on the floor and the crowd is disappearing à la *And Then There Were None*. Normally by the very end it'd be down to four people: Olivia Law (model), London Miller (model), Josie Bishop (beautiful hanger-on), and lightly freckled, moony-skinned, seventeen-year-old Eva-Kate Kelly.

Eva-Kate stood out among the others, mostly because she was so much more famous than they were. She was a child star turned party girl, one of the most gossiped-about actresses in Hollywood. She wasn't quite A-list, but almost. What I mean is that her work wasn't Oscar material, but America cherished her for what she gave them: easily digestible coming-of-age adventure features for the whole family.

Since 2007, when she'd appeared on the scene in *Jennie and Jenny*, it was clear that Eva-Kate Kelly was a prodigy. She was, at least in my mind, way too good for the club-kid scene she now dallied in, and I wondered why she chose to slum it with a motley crew of forgettable socialites. They'd be sprawled out on divans and daybeds with red eyes and blue tongues from sucking on lollipops all night and they'd look like hell, washed out and used up, and I knew I shouldn't want to be one of them but I did, because they were the main characters of this glittering train wreck, the center of Eva-Kate's world.

That night I was scrolling through the newest collection, titled "Sentiment Central." The party was inside what looked like a Swiss chalet filled up with white and silver balloons that bobbed around like detached heads. Many of the girls had bare arms and pastel lips and acrylic nails sharpened to a point like cat claws. The guys had overly styled goatees and baseball hats on backward and leather jackets revealing inky murals on their forearms. There was a photo of a girl with clear-rimmed glasses, tongue sticking out. There was a photo of that guy from *Breaking Bad*, the younger one, getting up close and personal with the camera, looking fake-confrontational. There was a photo of a Disney Channel actress with a champagne flute, holding it up like a trophy, a heavy, silvery chain bisecting the girl diagonally at her cleavage. Olivia, London, and Josie were there. Of course they were there, lazily leaning on one another, hair in faces, clinking glasses, blowing kisses. There was a photo of Olivia sitting on London's shoulders while Josie exhaled loose rings of smoke, hip cocked to the side, sapphire eyes fiercely glowing in the dark. There was a photo of London trying to put her hair in pigtails while flipping off the camera with one hand. There was a photo of Eva-Kate Kelly sharing a stick of purple rock candy with A-list singer-songwriter Rob Donovan, his hair perfectly pushed back in what was so obviously a tribute to James Dean it was almost more awkward than sexy. Almost.

About twenty-five photos in, the party moved outside to a pool surrounded by wet slate and wooden lounge chairs. Josie was the first to strip down to her Cosabella lace underwear and jump in. Others followed, and a game of chicken began. How many rounds of Marco Polo were played, I wondered, how many underwater tea parties? I clicked quickly through until the images began to take on motion and come to life like a flip-book: Olivia and London sat on the pool edge dipping their feet in the water, splashing it at each other, smoking cigarettes and staring off to the city sprawled out below.

Princess Leia barked—an endearingly ambitious bark—snapping me out of the fantasy and back onto my own porch with the dark canal water and the choiring crickets. My scene was a lonely one. Were it to be photographed, it would convey no motion and let off no heat, do you know what I mean? It would be cold and still like a block of ice. It would be silent. Which is not how a photograph of a sixteen-year-old should be. A photograph of a sixteen-year-old should burst with sound and warmth, energy and radiation drifting off the glossy sheet like the aftershocks of her adventures. I had no adventures. I went to a high school party once with Riley and Abbie but didn't know how to ask or answer the simplest questions and spent the night standing in a corner with half a flask of Jack Daniel's someone had handed me—too cautious to even taste it—watching girls in jean shorts rub their asses up against oblivious and undeserving dickheads. I carried around the feeling that something was definitely wrong with me, I just didn't know what. I'd never had sex. I couldn't even imagine it.

Yes, that's right: Despite what you've heard, when the summer of 2018 began, I was a virgin. The image they've fabricated of some kind of cold, calculating harlot is just that: a fabrication. And it couldn't be further from the truth.

Princess Leia barked again, her nose pointed and twitching at the house across the canal, a modern almost-mansion with tall windows, a smooth concrete exterior, and two fat palm trees sitting on either side. For as long as I could remember the house had been vacant; we'd easily been able to peer in and see how thoroughly un-lived-in it was inside, how empty. But then, suddenly one night, that night, it wasn't. Someone was in there.

"What?" I purred back at her. "What is it, my precious baby? Who's out there?" I looked out into the hedges that separated us from the still strip of water. "Who are you trying to protect us from, huh?"

That's when I saw her, my new neighbor. She walked across her living room, switching off lamps and lighting candles in their place. She opened a bottle of something and drank from it, then turned on the TV, which sprang to life in patches of fuzzy, rippled blue that filled up the room like water. It was almost as big as her wall, the TV was. Then there was me, watching from across the canal with the cookie dough I would soon be excavating for its chocolate chips, and Princess Leia, eyeing me suspiciously with each bite.

✻ ✻ ✻

The second time I saw her was seventeen hours later and in broad daylight. Princess Leia and I walked past the newly inhabited monstrosity-across-the-way for the third time that day when a girl came out to open her mailbox. She pulled open the tinny door and peered in, pouted, then slammed it shut. She turned toward me then and for a moment I was stunned: She wasn't just any new neighbor, she was Eva-Kate Kelly.

Yes, *the* Eva-Kate Kelly.

When people meet celebrities, they always say, "She was even more beautiful in person!" And yeah, Eva-Kate was more beautiful in person, but what struck me was how her face was so much more complex than on screen. It was somehow both narrow and full at the same time; her bones were delicate bird bones but her cheeks were two peaches sprayed with light freckles, and her eyes the glowing ends of optical fibers. When she saw me, she cocked her head to one side, the way Princess Leia would, and gave me a half smile with her orangey-red lips.

"Are you my new neighbor?" she asked. Her voice was deep for a girl's, but soft and airy. The words she spoke had space between them; they were loose and easy, caught in a breeze. My chest caved in on me. She took my breath away, she really did. I guess I have to admit that up front, otherwise there's no real point to writing all of this down for you (or for me?), no real point to getting the truth down on paper once and for all if I'm not being rigorously honest, right? Truth is multidimensional, that's one thing I've learned through all of this, and it spins like a planet thrown wildly out of orbit, making it hard to pin down. But I'm trying.

"I live over there," is what I finally said, "in that house," and pointed behind me, to the bungalow that sat perched in the massive shade cast by Eva-Kate's mansion.

"Lovely." She ran one index finger over the black velvet line of a choker around her pale neck. "I haven't met any neighbors yet, I only moved in yesterday so I haven't gotten to explore. I'm Eva-Kate, by the way."

She put out her hand for me to shake. It was icy cold.

"Yeah . . . I know," I said, then immediately regretted it. I'd made myself sound like a fangirl right off the bat, an outsider. But either she didn't notice or she didn't care.

"And you are?"

"I'm Justine."

"Justine . . . ?"

"Oh. Childs. Justine Childs."

"Well, Justine Childs"—she squeezed my hand—"I better get back to unpacking. It was nice to meet you, hope I'll be seeing you around."

She made a gun shape with her fingers and shot me with it.

I walked home trying to process what had just happened, trying to understand the somehow larger-than-life energy that emanated from her. She was one of those seemingly invincible people: I could imagine her driving drunk down Mulholland and emerging gracefully, more powerful than ever, sticking the landing like a skilled gymnast. And now she was my neighbor.

CHAPTER 7

I DON'T BELIEVE IT!

I spent that night watching Eva-Kate Kelly from my room, a low-ceilinged space with lots of wooden furniture painted white. From my window she was a blip, a radioactive presence inching across my screen. I found *Jennie and Jenny* on Netflix and made my way through the first season.

I had watched it as a kid, in the afternoons when my mom was seeing her patients and I had nothing to do. My dad would say do your homework, applying thick globs of paint to one of his canvases, a Corona in his free hand, and I'd say I already did (and I'd be telling the truth), and he'd turn to me with strained patience and say honey, I gotta work right now, can you find something to do until I'm finished and then I'll take you to the park? So I'd go into my room, close the door, and watch TV late into the night, falling asleep to the *Jennie and Jenny* opening theme song and Eva-Kate Kelly's ten-year-old voice vehemently declaring, "I don't believe it!"

Jennie and Jenny was a show about a ten-year-old who was part-time inhabited by her great-grandmother's spirit. Ordinarily, she was Jennie, hanging with her friends and being a regular, well-behaved kid. Then, once an episode, her mischievous, well-to-do, Prohibition-era great-grandmother, Jenny (who she was named for), would have a bone to pick with the way things were and would swoop down into Jennie's body to try to change it. More often than not, great-grandma Jenny felt that things in her descendants' lives were too dull, and she'd think of ways to shake things up, using her great-granddaughter as a vessel with which to do so. At least twice an episode, little Jennie would grip her own head and say, "I don't believe it!" and the live audience would go wild with laughter, maybe not at the line itself but at the precocious ten-year-old delivering the line with the self-aware charisma of an old soul. And thus, a catchphrase was born.

Looking back, I realize the show was essentially a kid-friendly portrayal of multiple personality disorder. For Jennie, being taken over by her great-grandmother was, in its best moments, funny, wacky, and, like, so weird (!). In its worst moments it was a total nuisance, and just like *uggghhhhh, so annoying*. Nothing like the actual experience of suffering from multiple personality disorder, which I'm sure is actually devastating and terrifying on a regular basis. Although there was that one episode where grandma Jenny has granddaughter Jennie lock herself in the basement of a building that was scheduled to be demolished in mere minutes. I forget her reasoning there, but I remember the nightmares it gave me.

I watched the first season, then the second, trying to reconcile the girl I had just met with the girl I'd watched on TV all those years ago. I'd look from my TV to the house across the canal and back again, as if doing so could connect the two versions of Eva-Kate Kelly and create something whole.

I felt creepy, like I was tracking her. But what was I tracking her for? What did I want from her? I wanted to be her friend, yes; I wanted her to want to be my friend. I stayed up late and searched her name on Google. I scrolled and scrolled. Eva-Kate Kelly at eight years old in stills from *Jennie and Jenny*, cheeks still plump with baby fat. Eva-Kate Kelly at eleven on the red carpet in a candy-colored two-piece dress, belly shamelessly exposed. Eva-Kate Kelly at thirteen on the red carpet in gray silk, hair pulled back in a chignon, a black leather clutch clutched tight, baby fat completely gone. Eva-Kate Kelly later the same year with her tongue sticking out, stained a shocking shade of blue you'd never find in nature (and if you did it would kill you). Eva-Kate Kelly at fourteen caught making out with sixteen-year-old pop star Rob Donovan on the shores of Zuma Beach. Eva-Kate Kelly at fifteen looking unconvincingly stoic in a yellow silk dress beneath stylistically uneven, asymmetrical lettering that read: EVA-KATE KELLY WANTS YOU TO KNOW YOU'RE NOT ALONE. IF YOU OR SOMEONE YOU KNOW IS HAVING SUICIDAL THOUGHTS, CALL 1-800-EKK-TALK. ONE HUNDRED PERCENT FREE AND CONFIDENTIAL. Eva-Kate Kelly floating on a blow-up pool chair with a blond bun on top of her head and Wildfox shades on her face and big neon print in the sky above her reading WHO IS THE REAL EVA-KATE KELLY? It felt like a valid question, but the accompanying article from three years ago talked only about how fourteen-year-old Eva-Kate saw herself as so much more than just an actress, about her jewelry line and her mission to end teenage suicide, about her crush on Kurt Cobain, and about her newfound passion for shabby chic sundresses.

✳ ✳ ✳

The next night Eva-Kate Kelly threw a party. Those noises, those colors. I'll never forget. They swarmed her home in the form of partygoers, riotous and thirsty, blue and purple klieg lights crisscrossing overhead, electronic music with a doped-up heartbeat pulsing deep in the water between us. Six times I went to my front door praying for the courage to cross the bridge and let myself in through Eva-Kate Kelly's front door, which was a mouth hung open, letting in fireflies. Fireflies wearing flower-patterned dresses and cork wedges, hair dyed pastel blue and pink and green. Fireflies in tracksuits. Fireflies in skinny jeans.

Even if I were brave enough to go, I had nothing to wear. My wardrobe consisted of Gap T-shirts and leggings, Converse All Stars with Beatles lyrics written in Sharpie on the white rubber soles, jean jackets with flowers embroidered, not ironically, on the cuffs and collars. So I went back to my room and laid myself down on this rug I had from IKEA that was in the shape of a big red spiral. I was the eye of the spiral with Princess Leia curled up on my chest and my hands over my ears, trying to block out the *nsst-nsst-nsst* and *bmp-bmp-bmp* sounds coming from across the water that were nothing more than sonic representations of my failure.

My phone rang—Night Owl, none of that default Marimba lameness—and the screen read MOM and I said to myself, out loud, "Agh, why????" but answered it anyway.

"Hi, Mom, I'm fine."

"Hi, my little ladybug, are you okay? How's Aunt Jillian? Remember to tell her to turn off the air-conditioning if it gets too cold."

"I said I'm fine. Yes. How are you? How's your—"

"What have you been eating? Make sure it's enough. I don't want to come home to find you wasted away."

"I'm eating enough," I said, chewing off a fingernail and spitting it out.

"I hope so. How's Princess Leia?"

"Perfect." I didn't mention that she'd been trying to run away, that I'd caught her trying to burrow under the front gate twice now. "Do you want to talk to her?" I put the phone to Princess Leia's wet mouth and waited about five seconds, then brought it back to my own mouth and said, "Sorry, I guess she doesn't want to talk."

"Very funny, Justine. Are you walking her?"

"Every day."

"*Twice* every day."

"Right, yeah. Twice every day."

"And what about sunscreen?"

"Oh my God, Mom, what *about* sunscreen?"

"Are you wearing it? I read that UV rays have never been higher than they are right now. Or maybe it was that they've never been *stronger* than they are right now. Well, either way, they've never been more *something* as they are right now. You can get skin cancer just by going outside if you're not careful. SPF 50, at least."

"Got it."

"And is Jillian taking you home to check the mail?"

"Uh . . . sure." I peered outside at the tin mailbox with that useless red arrow switched to an upright position. "Yeah."

"Justine, you have to check the mail, it isn't going to kill you. If you're going to be weird about opening it, fine, but you have to get Jillian to drive you home so you can bring it *into the house*, otherwise when burglars come snooping by they'll see mail piling up and think no one's home. It's just an open invitation for them to have a field day."

"Okay, okay. I'll bring the mail in." I wasn't going to do it, though. Mail triggered a sense of unease within me that I just didn't need right now.

"I have one more thing to ask you but I think you'll just bite my head off. Promise not to bite my head off?"

"You're on the other side of the world, I couldn't even if I tried."

"You seem like you're getting . . . moody again. Are you taking your meds?"

"Of course I am, why wouldn't I be?"

"You can be forgetful sometimes. I would just hate for you to end up—well, no offense, honey, but you know."

"Yep. I know."

"Remember to call Dr. Campbell if you need refills."

"I will. Mom, I gotta go, is there anything else?"

"Have you heard from your dad?"

"Nope."

"Really? He said he'd call you."

"Hasn't yet."

"I'll make sure he does."

"No need. Really. Love you, Mom, call whenever, okay? I'll be here."

"Bye, angel face. Remember the SPF! Less than 50

won't do anything for you. But check the bottle for parabens first, you *have* to check for parabens, otherwise you might as well not wear anythi—"

I hung up and said "Goddammit" to myself, but out loud, then hurried to my feet because the truth was I had run out of my various meds five days ago and had forgotten to get them refilled. I *could* be forgetful, she was right. I pulled a Santa Monica Symphony Orchestra sweater over my pajamas and clipped a leash onto Princess Leia's collar. I had an hour and fifteen minutes until the pharmacy closed.

✳ ✳ ✳

With its fluorescents and glittering linoleum, the Walgreens on Lincoln Boulevard was the definition of a clean, well-lighted place. For that reason, I felt extremely safe there. Even with the homeless men just outside who towered above me red-faced and practically drenched in cheap vodka. I walked down the middle aisle past rows of brightly packaged razor blades tightly held behind lock and key to the pharmacy where Ruth, in a white medical jacket, saw me coming and unhooked my plastic medication bags off the rack, started ringing them up one by one. Ruth and I were so practiced at this routine that we could do the whole thing without speaking once: credit, yes, I decline to be counseled by a pharmacist, yes, signature, enter, cue receipt print. She put the receipt into a white paper bag with my meds and folded it up neatly, handed it to me with that matte pink smile of hers and a nod.

"Oh, oh, and did I tell you?" A girl in athleisure wear was speaking to another girl in athleisure wear (maybe in their early twenties) near the blood pressure machine with shopping baskets hanging from the crooks of their elbows. Spandex-cotton-hybrid leggings enveloping their sculpted bubble butts, hair wrapped up high in messy buns tied with flat cotton-candy-colored bands. TOMS shoes. Both had nude gel manicures.

"Tell me what?" This girl was wearing blue leggings and an array of rose-gold bangles.

"Guess who moved to Venice?" This one was wearing black leggings and a bronze anklet around her bronze ankle.

"Who?" Blue Leggings asked.

"Eva-Kate Kelly," Black Leggings said deviously, clearly expecting a reaction.

"Oh, duh. I knew that."

"And you didn't tell me?"

"I thought everyone knew."

"*I* didn't."

"Why do you care so much?"

"Don't you remember? She slept with Blake. My *ex-boyfriend* Blake. While we were still together." Black Leggings pouted.

"Isn't she like twelve?" Blue Leggings asked.

"Seventeen now. And kind of a slut."

"So, what? You're worried now she lives in town she's gonna steal your new bae?"

"She wishes," Black Leggings said with a tinge of concern.

"I dunno, man, she *did* just break up with Rob Donovan."

"So?"

"So she's single and at large. Probably looking for a rebound to mend her broken heart."

"Oh please, she's not brokenhearted, they break up and get back together every five minutes."

"I heard this time's different."

"Different how?"

"I heard this time he broke up with her because he fell in love with another girl."

"Really? Who?"

"Liza."

"Liza . . . as in *Liza McKelvoy*?" Black Leggings gripped on to her shopping basket with both hands.

"Yes," Blue Leggings assured her, caring a whole lot less.

"No!"

"Yes!"

"Liza fucking McKelvoy? Damn, Eva-Kate must hate that. She must be losing her mind."

"Probably."

"*Oh my God.*" Black Leggings shook her head and exclaimed, "*I don't believe it!*" Then the two broke out in a fit of infectious—dare I say malicious—laughter.

I realized I was eavesdropping and receiving information I didn't want. I slipped away into the open and elegant aisles of Walgreens and surveyed it like a kingdom.

The way Audrey Hepburn in *Breakfast at Tiffany's* feels about Tiffany's, that's how I felt—and still do feel—about Walgreens. Nothing very bad can happen in the aisles of Walgreens. I could block out whatever unsettling gossip I had just heard in Walgreens. I walked with Princess Leia past my favorite attractions:

1. The boundless array of hair care products—Pantene to Paul Mitchell to Kérastase—each one promising some form of damage repair or healing properties, the word *miracle* written frequently, most often in gold.

2. The oral hygiene aisle, almost entirely white, rows of tubes and bottles and boxes that looked like teeth, promising death to germs, radical, inhuman levels of cleanliness, and most importantly, the promise of WHITE, WHITE, WHITE.

3. The face wash aisle bursting with the names and colors of exotic fruits, exotic chemicals. WITH this, WITHOUT that, the labels bragged. Promises of tightened pores and speedy zit reduction and miracle wrinkle zapping. That *miracle* word again. So many miracles, so many promises. I didn't care to find out if they'd hold up. I didn't have money to buy these products, so I was perpetually in a state of having promises being made to me and never experiencing the heartache of having them broken.

See, the zoned-out tranquillity bubble I achieved from roaming the Walgreens floor plan would be popped instantly were I to buy anything. If I bought anything I'd have to go up front to the cash registers, where an infantry of fashion magazines stood tall and proud, displaying the faultless faces of those with fresh fame in various evening-gown-and-diamond combinations, in various power stances and/or elegantly abstract hand poses. Nothing in this life makes me feel so hopeless as these A-list celebs with their big, glossy magenta mouths and their immaculate, satiny skin. They were the gorgeous gargoyles guarding the entrance to Celebrityland, refusing to let me in.

I walked home in the dark with Rob Donovan's "Your Secret Paradise" stuck in my head and wondered if what I'd heard was true. Had he left Eva-Kate for another girl? Did she hate it? Was she losing her mind? She'd seemed fine to me. What did those girls know, anyway? Eva-Kate Kelly wasn't the type to get her heart broken, she had more important things to do. Those girls were misinformed, I decided, and resented them on Eva-Kate's behalf.

CHAPTER 8

DGAF

(Or, Kanye West and Taylor Swift Will Never Have Sex. Like, Ever.)

*I*n a dream, a furiously gloomy dream in translucent shades of green, I was following Eva-Kate out onto the end of the Santa Monica Pier. She wasn't afraid to step among the rusty hooks and fish guts. She looked out onto the mossy ocean and drained it like Moses. Then she jumped. I woke up sweaty, sick with the feeling that I had lost her.

It took me a moment to get back to reality, and when I did I decided I needed a bath. Our bathtub was Pepto Bismol pink. The tiles around the tub had cracks running through them and the cracks had dirt and mold running through them. I hated this, it made me feel so dirty, but no matter how hard I scrubbed, the dirt always reaccumulated, the mold and moss always grew back. I liked my bathwater scalding hot to the point where I thought maybe it was actually cold, where the water was so hot that it set my nerves ablaze and all I felt was a tingling, buzzing sensation like a million simultaneous pinpricks. It was the exact type of intensity and confusion I needed to shut my mind off, to make me forget the hooks and the fish guts, that I had lost Eva-Kate Kelly, that she was a seventeen-year-old with a mansion and a face that had been broadcast across the planet, that maybe if you think something is true and believe it is true, then it is true. Like my mom: She was having an affair with a patient but telling herself that she wasn't cheating on my dad. She said if a tree fell in the woods and nobody was around to hear it fall, it did not make a sound, and took this to mean that if she had sex with her patient but nobody ever found out about it, then it didn't happen. Of course then I found out, and that's when she explained all this to me, while I sat nestled deep into the couch in her office, like I was just another one of her many patients whose minds she was paid to professionally iron out.

When I started thinking like this, suddenly there would be no up and no down, and I'd gradually, day by day, feel more and more like a sentence written down at the bottom corner of a page, jumbled and slippery and in danger of sliding right off. So I tried to keep straight with the truth, stay on good terms with reality, because let's just say for now that it was real unpleasant the one time it got away from me.

* * *

Anyway, so I was in the bath and I could see these plump juicy clouds outside the window, dark and marbled, and I hoped it would rain. I remember this because I remember everything about that day, and I remember everything about that day because it was made up of what I now consider to be my last mundane moments of life. I didn't know it then, but I was about to slip off the bottom of the page and into an incoherent vastness of supernovas, ultraviolet and infrared bursts of gaseous light, nothing solid or substantial to grip or grab on to. Imagine Alice falling down the rabbit hole and the moment she begins to wonder if her feet will touch ground ever again after all.

I washed my hair and soaked until my fingers wrinkled, then drained the tub and dried off, wrapped myself in a fuzzy purple robe from Old Navy. Despite the hot bath, my mind was still reeling, sizzling, so I put *Gossip Girl* on the living room flat screen and tried to zone out. I watched all of season one while eating a full tube of chocolate chip cookie dough and then cleaned the entire house from top to bottom. I used Lysol and Clorox bleach to scrub down all the surfaces and tried to imagine that advertised 99.99 percent of bacteria burning up on contact. I spent the day like that. I microwaved a burrito and then forgot to eat it. I deleted 433 photos from my phone that were taking up unnecessary space. I brushed Princess Leia's hair. I read an article in *Nylon* magazine called "Twenty Other Girls Under Twenty." I ordered a unicorn-shaped phone cover online using my mom's credit card she left for me to use in emergencies. I watched the sunset from my bedroom window with Princess Leia and tried to listen for the crickets that hid out in the wires and woodwork. Princess Leia heard them and tried fruitlessly to hunt them down.

I was so tired from trying not to think all day, and with the sun down and a sugar crash coming on and the cricket lullaby, it was becoming less and less appealing to keep my eyes open. But according to the clock it was barely eight thirty and so I couldn't go to sleep just yet, it would have been too sad. So I got my MacBook and started looking through I Know What You Did Last Night. It was a newly posted set called "Hot Mess Time Machine" that took place at an upscale karaoke bar with red leather couches and gold-framed record covers from the eighties on the walls. There was an Emma Stone look-alike in black leather pants posing with a bright magenta-colored drink, and then an Emily Ratajkowski look-alike in a Rolling Stones T-shirt (or maybe it actually was Emily Ratajkowski, the real one) singing into a microphone while the lyrics to "Hold Me Now" by the Thompson Twins appeared on a bright blue screen to her right. The next photo was of Eva-Kate, by this point a familiar face, but I felt like I was looking at her for the first time, actually *seeing* her now. She wore a hat with a wide brim that hid her eyes so that her pale glitter-glossed lips, the black velvet choker around a slender blue-white neck, were the focal point of the shot. She wore a black fur coat over a leotard with skeleton ribs painted on. She was juvenile, vulnerable but 100 percent carefree among a sea of veteran socialites with practiced poses and cooperative fabric patterns. She herself had all the experience necessary to photograph like holier-than-thou Hollywood royalty, but she chose not to. She went about the party acting like each camera flash had caught her off guard, and as a result in pictures she looked clumsy and unprepared, like a newborn deer. And just like a newborn deer, her aesthetic came off as adorable and charming. She knew what she was doing.

✳ ✳ ✳

Just then an eruption of music bounded over the waterway. I went to the window and saw a trail of neon and suede filtering into the front gate of Eva-Kate Kelly's mansion just across the canal. I glanced compulsively at my phone (a quick and easy comfort in the face of insecurity) and was surprised to see that it was ten o'clock. Two hours had passed since I first wanted to go to bed. How long had I been staring into the computer screen?

Where had that time gone? And where was Princess Leia?

"Princess!" I called out, seeing that she wasn't in my bedroom with me anymore. "Princess Leia!" I walked out into the living room and found her stuck hanging halfway out the window. She had to have hopped up onto the coffee table to reach, but then couldn't fit all the way through the opening in the glass where night air was now slithering in ribbons.

"Yo. Girlfriend. Are you serious?" I laughed, scooped her up by the belly, and set her back down on the hardwood floor. She looked up at me with her mouth open and tongue hanging out, tail wagging slowly back and forth. It wasn't an excited tail wag, it was a hopeful tail wag, one that said "I hope you're not mad at me for trying to sneak out again." Like a teenager who had waited for Mom and Dad to fall asleep before she snuck out in search of that big world outside. Like I should be doing. How was it that I ended up the one kid who didn't have any parents to try to sneak away from and no legitimate reason for staying in?

"Come on, we're getting ready for bed," I said to her, and she followed obediently to my room, then curled up on the red-ringed rug and sighed deeply. I left my curtains open while I changed into baby-blue pajamas, not because I'm some sort of twisted exhibitionist but because the thought of closing them—the thought of hiding my body from the world—just hadn't ever crossed my mind. For a sixteen-year-old girl, I dwelled very little on my appearance. I watched my friends vying for male attention and felt bored. I couldn't figure out why they scrutinized themselves, dutifully altered themselves on a daily basis, just so that some boy might or might not lust after them. As if somehow male attraction increased our value! As if their gazes could validate us! I mean, had girls *seen* the guys at our school? Surely these gangly mini-men with bad skin and body odor and generic-as-hell fashion sense were not qualified to glance in our direction, let alone determine how we felt about ourselves.

Don't get me wrong, it's not like I was Queen Confidence when it came to body image, I just didn't spend much time thinking about it one way or the other. My whole life people had called me pretty, and I'd agreed with them. I figured if as a girl my job was to look pretty, then my work there was done. And, when it came to boys, the very last thing I wanted was extra credit.

"Man I can understand how it might be kinda hard to love a girl like me." Rihanna's voice recorded over synth organ reached me from across the canal, the opening lyrics to Kanye West's "Famous." The beat dropped and Kanye started in.

I used to be a Kanye West fan. *The College Dropout, Late Registration, Graduation* . . . I was all about these albums. When he called himself an artist and a genius, I agreed with him. I still agree with him, actually, but this lyric from "Famous" and the reignited feud that followed kinda broke my heart. For those of you who don't remember: In 2009, Taylor Swift's "You Belong with Me" won Best Music Video at the VMAs, and when she went to accept her award, Kanye drunkenly took the mic from her and said, "Imma let you finish, but Beyoncé had one of the best music videos of all time." Nineteen-year-old Taylor went backstage and cried, but soon after, he apologized, and in her then-magnanimous heart, she forgave him. Seven years later, as the story goes, Kanye called her up and asked if he could use her name in a song. She gave him her blessing. But when the song came out on his 2016 album, *The Life of Pablo*, she was horrified. Yes, she'd given him her permission to use her name, but never did she approve of him claiming that he "made that bitch famous." The internet lashed out at Taylor, calling her a liar and a hypocrite for giving her blessing and then acting like she hadn't. This attack on Taylor was majorly unfair. It is one thing to use her name in a song and another thing entirely to degrade her as a woman and attempt to undermine her success as one of the most essential pop stars of our time. And, my personal opinion: How dare he pretend that interrupting her award speech was the cause of her fame. Where was he in 2008 when she was nominated for Female Vocalist of the Year at the Country Music Awards, or when she won Country

Female Artist that same year at the American Music Awards? What about 2010 when *Fearless* won Album of the Year at the Grammys? And besides, if he made her famous by stealing the spotlight that night, then how'd she get up on stage—beating out Beyoncé for Best Music Video—in the first place? Oh right, because she was already famous.

And don't get me started on the phone call that dug up all this buried drama. If Kanye had called Taylor up for an innocent chat, a courtesy call between friends, then why did he have his *wife* record it? If you guessed because he intended to set Taylor up from the beginning, then you're correct. He knew she'd approve on the spot and he knew that when he released the altered version she would react negatively on a public level and then he'd be able to swoop in with his little recording and make her look like a sneaky bitch trying to use him to elevate her public image as an innocent—albeit tenacious and unbreakable—victim. By releasing the video of her condoning the lyric "me and Taylor might still have sex," Kanye and the ever-loathsome Kim Kardashian made it look like Taylor had secretly given him her blessing, only to publicly shame him for it later on. So, if you can follow: They plotted to make her look bad by setting her up to look like she had plotted to make him look bad. And they call *her* the snake? No, no. Make no mistake, true snakes in this story wear Yeezys.

Riley and Maddie and Abbie told me I couldn't say this out loud, or people might think I'm racist. That's the problem one can get into when trying to parse out who's to blame in the #KanTay feud. If you blame Kanye, you're racist. If you blame Taylor, you're sexist. It's actually pretty disrespectful to both of them, reducing their experiences down to race and gender like that. They're both just people, after all. Both more famous than God, but still, just people.

Anyway, when all is said and done, the joke's on Kanye. If he hadn't fucked up so badly this time around with the shadiest phone call of all time, we might not have been blessed with the gift that is *Reputation*. Look what you made her do, indeed.

P.S. Kim, are you okay? Your husband writes a song about having sex with Taylor Swift and you respond by helping him take down her career?

P.P.S. I'd start a #SaveKim hashtag if I didn't suspect the three of them were coconspirators in this publicity stunt the whole time.

P.P.P.S. Prove to me their managers didn't hatch this entire plan way back on the eve of the 2009 VMAs.

✳ ✳ ✳

Now, as his blasphemous song blasted across the canal, I heard, beneath the rapping and whooping, beneath the drum machine, the sound of toenails scratching against glass. I swung around to the rug and, of course, Her Royal Highness was gone again. I ran out into the living room, this time just as Princess Leia was wriggling out the front window. She jumped out and hit the ground running.

"Dammit!" I clenched my fists, still only half dressed, and cursed myself for not closing the window after her first attempt. "Get back here!" I called out in vain. She ran up to the opening in our chain-link fence and easily darted through. I hurried my legs into the pajama bottoms, grabbed a sweater, and ran after her; there was nothing else I could do. She had at least fifteen feet on me as I chased her down the canal sidewalk, thinking what the hell was this dog running from and where the hell did she think she was going? She trotted across the footbridge, toward the party at Eva-Kate's. I envied her dumb confidence. She didn't know or care that we weren't, as fate would have it, among the teen elite, and therefore had no place showing up here, uninvited. She didn't know or care. But I knew and I cared, and so I tried one last time to catch up with her before it was too late. I failed, and then it was too late: I saw her curly white, lamblike coat disappear into the hedges of 18 Carroll Canal.

Oh my God, I felt so completely, helplessly screwed. I

mean, can you imagine? It's almost eleven at night and I'm standing there—barefoot, mind you—in pajamas, everything completely dark except for the supernova of lights coming from Eva-Kate's backyard, blending from blue into purple into pink into white. I had to go in. I didn't want to go in, but I had to. *It doesn't matter if Eva-Kate Kelly thinks you look dumb and sadly juvenile in your pajamas*, I had to tell myself. *If you lose Princess Leia you'll never forgive yourself.*

So I walked in through her ivy-covered archway and sighed deeply: There was Princess Leia sniffing a row of potted plants that lined the front door, which was slightly ajar. I stepped lightly across the dewy lawn, but I was too slow; before I could reach her, she ducked behind the door, disappearing into the house. This time I followed her in without thinking, my mind a slate made blank by panic.

Then the turquoise hit. A wall of it, a room of it. Turquoise velvet couches and turquoise-tinted table glass, turquoise damask rug and turquoise fleur-de-lis curtains. So much turquoise that I almost didn't notice the two girls, each in their own version of the Little Black Dress, one sitting cross-legged on the couch and the other facing her on the turquoise wood ottoman, deep in conversation, champagne flutes in hand. I recognized them from the website as London Miller and Olivia Law.

"Excuse me?" I cleared my throat. "Did either of you

see a dog run through here?" They turned their heads wearily upward to look at me.

"Oh, was that *your* dog?" Olivia said. Her dark brown hair was piled on top of her head and held in place with a clip shaped like an eagle talon.

"What a precious little angel," said London, pointing into the next room. "She went that way." Her hair was long and reddish, stick-straight, conditioned to the point of perfection.

"I thought she went that way." Olivia pointed up at a wrought iron spiral staircase.

"No, no, she definitely went that way." London pressed one finger against her lips. "Or maybe . . . you know, I don't think I can say for sure which way she went."

"We weren't paying close attention."

"Sorry."

"Yeah, sorry." Neither of them seemed even slightly sorry as they turned to face each other and continued talking closely. I thanked them, though I don't think they heard me, and chose to go with the first direction, which was through a second door into a room that was almost as pink as the first room was turquoise.

This room was three or four times larger than the first; and seemed to be more of an attraction than a place to live. People gathered in the center, playing pool on a pink-felt pool table, or waited in line to ride a kiddy carousel—the kind you put quarters into outside of grocery stores—in the back corner, or stood around dancing loosely and without commitment to a pumped-up remix of "Still D.R.E." by Dr. Dre featuring Snoop Dogg. Security cameras hung from each corner of the wall, roving back and forth. The room was crowded; if Princess Leia was in there, I would have had no way of knowing. I walked through slowly, with my eyes on the floor, trying to look for her, trying not to be seen, while also trying not to have my bare toes stepped on by a mob of Manolo Blahniks and Jeffrey Campbells and Doc Martens and tooth-white Adidas. In one corner I noticed a cookie jar stuffed with not cookies but Red Vines licorice. At another time I would have stopped to take one (or two), but I was on a mission.

The room came to an end in a wall of glass that slid open into the backyard. That's where the real party was. Mosaic tables in every corner supported rows and rows of mojitos for guests to swoop up and gulp down. When the tables emptied off, caterers filed in to replace and refill, so that the river of minty syrup and rum could remain in a lush state of perpetual motion. In the center of the backyard, in the middle of all the drunk-ish, ultra-pretty partygoers, was a pool surrounded by an oasis of palm trees, each fixed with lights that shifted from color to color, as I'd seen from the street. I walked into the ring of trees and was surprised to see people actually in the pool, some swimming, some sprawled out on the marble rim, wet underwear cling-ing to their skin.

"Hey!" a guy, mostly submerged, called out from the pool. "Why are you wearing pajamas?" It took me a moment before I realized he was talking to me, that I had been seen, found out.

"Oh, I, uh—I'm looking for my dog, actually. Have you seen her? She's white, fluffy—"

"She was here a minute ago," the guy said, dazed, one hand resting on his wet head. "Eva-Kate just took her upstairs."

Was I relieved that Princess Leia was safe? Yes, sure. But I felt panicky nonetheless. I was in no position to see Eva-Kate Kelly right then, let alone speak to her; I was in my pajamas and my hair was surely disheveled from navigating through her sumptuous home. But what was I going to do, let her keep Princess Leia forever?

"Could you tell me how to get upstairs?" I asked.

"Try going up the stairs." One girl, half-naked, smirked, and her friends giggled along.

"Fine, great. Thanks." I blushed, I'm sure I did, then retraced my steps back to the first room with the wrought iron spiral staircase, where London and Olivia were now snorting lines of white powder off the semi-reflective, turquoise-tinted coffee table.

At the top of the staircase I followed a long hallway lined with closed doors to the one open door at the very end where more people were gathered. Just outside the door was a clear plastic corded phone, the kind from the early 2000s where you could see all the hot-pink and green inner gears and electronics. Next to it was a matching answering machine, which I'd never actually seen before but recognized from descriptions in stories my parents told.

The energy upstairs was nothing like the energy downstairs. The music was low, slow beats and strong bass beating like a heart buried deep in the walls. Nobody danced. Everybody lounged on Moroccan rugs and suede beanbag chairs, passing around what looked like a metal pen connected to cloth tubing connected to a glass vase. The air smelled like Red Vines.

Peering over their heads, I saw Eva-Kate reclining on a canopy bed with Princess Leia tucked into the crook of her elbow. Since the last time I'd seen her, she'd chopped her hair to just under her chin and dyed it cotton-candy pink. She saw me standing in the doorway and sat up straight, crossed her legs, and smiled like she had been expecting me.

"Justine, right?" she asked. I nodded. "Justine, look who found me!" She kissed the top of Princess Leia's head.

"She snuck out," I said, almost out of breath by this point. "Sorry. I've been trying to chase her down."

"What a bad girl!" Eva-Kate cupped Leia's cheeks in

her palms, delighted. "I mean the dog, not you, obviously," she said, turning to me, winking. "Although they say dogs take after their masters, so ya never know." The word *master* in her mouth had a devious weight to it.

"I'll get her out of your way now." I walked over and scooped Princess Leia off the bed. "Sorry to interrupt your party. You have an awesome home. But you already know that." My face was heating up, I hoped not visibly. "Anyway, have a great night, I'll see you around. The neighborhood."

"No, no, you just got here! Stay."

"What?" I know I must have sounded rude, my blunt, stunned question dropping to the floor like lead. But Eva-Kate didn't flinch.

"Sit down, sit down. Can I get you a drink?"

"I'm . . . in my pajamas."

"So? You look totally adorbs, trust me. This look is so DGAF."

"DGAF?"

"Don't Give A Fuck? As in, I don't give a fuck, I'll wear pajamas to a party at Eva-Kate Kelly's house if I want."

"Oh." I felt stupefied in her presence.

"Sit down, sit down," she said again, patting a spot for me on the bed. I did as she said, hesitantly, setting Princess Leia on my lap and gripping her tight for comfort. "Oh my God." She rested her hand lightly on my knee then. "Look at your poor feet. What happened?" I didn't know what she meant. I looked down at my poor feet and saw: They were scraped and bleeding, dirty with the patterns of various soles.

"Jesus." I felt very detached from my feet then; I couldn't feel their pain. "I had to run over here barefoot because Princess Leia—that's the dog—jumped out the window and I didn't have time to put on shoes. Then I was looking for her downstairs and I guess people stepped on my toes." I laughed. "Which is so weird because I didn't even notice. I was too focused on finding Princess Leia and getting the hell out of here."

"Why would you want to get the hell out of here?" She looked hurt, and I felt an immediate horror at myself for causing her even the slightest sliver of pain.

"No, no, I mean because I wasn't invited. And I didn't want you to think I was crashing your party, I mean, I didn't mean to crash your party, I was just—"

"But you *were* invited."

"I was?"

"I put an invitation in your mailbox. Two invitations, actually, one for tonight and one for last night."

I hadn't checked the mail in over a week. I told you already about how I feel about mail: Nothing good ever comes from checking it. Until now, I guess, had I checked it.

"I haven't been opening my mail," I said with my head

low, as if this were something to be ashamed of. When I think about it now, I realize that in those days I could feel shame about almost anything.

"That's a relief. I was almost starting to think you were snubbing me. Josie!" she called over her shoulder. "Do we have shoes?"

Josie, a tall and almost awkwardly thin girl with careless honey-blond hair, wearing a purple sundress and leather jacket, looked up from her cross-legged seat on the floor. Despite her dress and flower-child-flowing hair, there was something boyish about her. It was in the way she sat, hunched gracelessly as if trying to make room for her long arms.

"Do we have *shoes*?" she asked, her voice husky, impressively raising one eyebrow away from the other. Her face was striking in an androgynous way; with short hair and a different outfit, she could have been a beautiful boy.

"*Extra* shoes," she said to Josie, then turned back to me. "What size do you wear?"

"Me? Oh, like a seven?"

"Josie, could you just check to see if we have any size seven shoes in the second closet?"

"You got it, babe." Josie dusted her hands off and walked into what I presumed was the second closet in the back of the room.

"Josie is my personal assistant," Eva-Kate said to me.

"But also my actual best friend; I'd literally die without her."

Ah, yes, I can't live without my personal assistant either, I wanted to say. I pressed my lips together and nodded.

"Companies send me shoes and clothes and bags all the time but normally it's just stuff I would never wear so I throw it all in the second closet. We'll find you something."

"That's incredibly sweet and unnecessary of you."

"Totally necessary. I can't let my best neighbor go around with cold, beat-up feet. I'm not a monster."

Josie came back holding a white shoe box that read PATRICIA GREEN, and opened it up to reveal a pair of petal-pink slippers with the Eiffel Tower embroidered on the fronts.

"This is all you have in a seven," she said to Eva-Kate while she handed me the open box.

"Perfect." Eva-Kate sat back, seemingly pleased with herself. "Those go with your loungewear vibes." I thanked them both and slipped my feet into the pink velour.

"You know what? I'm bored." Eva-Kate used her long fingernails to grip on to a Red Vine and slide it out of its packaging. "This party's getting dull. Let's go to the roof." She bit into the Red Vine and chewed it delicately.

"Okay . . . yeah, sure," I said, scooping Princess Leia up off the bed.

Eva-Kate linked her arm through mine and led me to the other end of the hall, where there was a fire escape that matched the wrought iron spiral staircase I had climbed up. It wasn't much of an escape, though, as it only connected the upstairs hallway window to the roof.

"There are so many morons at this party and you're the only one I actually want to talk to," she said, pushing open the window, with the hand that wasn't holding on to that singular Red Vine. "My roof is a great place to get to know someone. You'll see."

"Why me? I mean, what do you want to talk to me about?"

"First of all, there's the fact that we live right across from each other; don't you think that means the universe wanted us to be friends?" She climbed the staircase and I followed, not sure if the heartbeat racing against my chest was mine or Princess Leia's.

"Oh, sure," I said. "I hadn't thought of that." Though of course, I had.

"Second of all, you're just like this quiet, down-to-earth mystery girl who doesn't open her mail. I feel like I want to figure you out, find out what other things you're weird about."

Me? Mystery girl? Yeah, right. And yeah, maybe I'm "down to earth," but that's only when my meds are working.

"And third of all, I know you've been watching me."

My heart sank. We were almost at the top of the staircase, but in that moment I thought seriously about backing down, leaving Princess Leia, moving to Canada, changing my name. Instead, I held on to the iron railing.

"How?" I asked. "How do you know that?"

"Because," she said, reaching for my hand to pull me up onto the roof, "I've been watching you too."

CHAPTER 9

SILVER LIPS

*S*tanding on Eva-Kate Kelly's rooftop then, we had a perfect view across the canal into my own bedroom window. I couldn't believe it: From up there she could see the most private part of my life. From up there she could watch me more closely and more intimately even than I had watched her.

"I don't . . ." I wanted to say, *I don't understand*, I wanted to say, *Why would you bother?* But the words felt heavy, weighted down to my tongue. Maybe I should have felt violated, but all I felt was flattered, and then excitement too big for my body.

"It's not like I was trying to spy on you." She stood up straight with her shoulders back, her small breasts pushed up and out. I'd never seen anyone with such impeccable posture. *She must have been a dancer, I* thought, *earlier on in life. There's no way Rob Donovan left her,* I thought, *why would he? Just look at her . . .* "It's just, I come up here a lot to do my crystals and one day I looked over and there you were with your little face in the window, and you were looking for me, I could tell. You were scanning my house, wanting to see me. You didn't know I was up on the roof, you didn't think to look up here." She giggled. "I don't know if you could even see up here from down there, you'll have to check and tell me once you get home."

"This is the most embarrassed I've ever been in my whole life," I scrambled to explain. "I can't believe you saw—I mean, you know, I wasn't trying to spy on you either. I've lived here my whole life and this house has been empty for years and I was super curious to see who had finally moved in." I spoke fast, there was no way I could explain myself fast enough. I would have done anything then to convince her I wasn't a total psycho. The fact that she had been guilty of the exact same thing had slid greasily away from me like water off a duck's back. Under the moonlight her kimono looked silvery and liquid.

"Oh, relax," she said. "As if I care. You have no reason to be embarrassed. What's a little curiosity between neighbors?"

I nodded, my cheeks still burning. I was relieved she saw it that way, but the subject felt distantly dirty and I wanted very badly to move off it.

"So, what do you mean you come up here to 'do crystals'?"

"Oh my God." She touched my forearm with the wilting Red Vine wand. "You must have thought I was talking about drugs. It sounds like drugs when you say it. But no, I don't do drugs. Well, I mean, I don't do crystal meth. Gross, could you imagine?" She cringed painfully and stroked her cheek like it was her most prized possession and she couldn't bear the thought of losing it to a flesh-ravaging substance. I didn't blame her, her skin was prize-worthy: naturally flushed and luminous with just the right amount of moisture, practically poreless. "I'm talking about, like, actual crystals. Rose quartz, amethyst, opal, onyx, tiger eye, tourmaline. Selenite. My healer has me lie naked in the sunlight with the crystals placed on different parts of my body. For healing purposes, of course, it's nothing perverted, promise."

"I believe you," I said, trying not to picture her naked body splayed out on the roof.

"You have to try it sometime, it's incredible. The sunlight magnifies and intensifies the crystal's healing properties, so like every part of you feels sooo good afterward. They fortify your bones and organs and stuff so you just feel so alive, but also like very protected, you know? I mean, I don't know if you believe in that stuff, but you'll try it and then you'll see: It works. Will you try it?"

"Absolutely."

"I'll introduce you to my healer. Her name's Ruby and she just knows everything about crystals and astrology. She's practically a witch. You'll love her."

"Awesome," I said, trying hard to sound casual, overly critical of every sound that left my mouth.

"So, what's your deal? Can I ask you that?"

I glanced down at Princess Leia, whose eyes were starting to droop.

"Me? What do you mean?"

"No, the dog." She rolled her eyes. "Yes, you, dummy. Who are you? Who do you want to be? Are you happy or sad? Are you lonely and if so why? Are you in love?" As she spoke, she walked to the far corner of the roof where there were two gray canvas lounge chairs and dragged them over to us. "Let's relax a little, I'm not a gigantic fan of standing on my feet." She stretched out on the chair and I followed her lead. I wondered if it was her fame and early-in-life money that attributed to her poised confidence, or if it was something she had developed before. Or could it have been something she was born with? Whatever the answer, it was something I didn't have, something I coveted and marveled at as if it were Le Coeur de la Mer.

"I don't know where to begin," I confessed. "I'm not sad, I know that much . . . but I'm not happy. I don't think I really know what it means to be happy. And I've never been in love."

"What about your parents?"

"What about them?"

"Are they in love?"

"Oh. No. They're in the middle of a divorce. Well, no, not in the middle. They're at the very beginning of getting a divorce."

"Is that why they're never around? In the whole time I've been living here I haven't seen them once."

"My mom is traveling. She'll be back in a month. My dad moved to the Valley. He calls it North Hollywood, but it's really the Valley. What about your parents, what do they think of—"

"We're not doing me tonight." She shook her head. "I want to hear all about you."

"No, you don't," I assured her. "Your life is at least ten times more interesting than mine, I promise you."

"I'm a snooze fest." She rolled her eyes and swatted at me violently. "I'm the worst. That's why I throw these parties, because most days I honestly don't have anything else to do."

"And you think I do have anything interesting to do? It's summer vacation and my parents left me alone. Without a car, mind you."

"So you clean. Compulsively."

"Oh God. I forgot you've seen me."

"And you sleep."

"Uh-huh." With crossed arms, I raised my shoulders up to my ears, as if that could make my head disappear.

"And you walk around in your underwear."

"Oh my God, stop!" I hid my face in my hands, mortified.

"Don't be embarrassed, crazy! You have an amazing body. I wish I had that body."

"*My* body?"

"Are you kidding me? I would kill for your boobs."

"Be my guest, they're probably just weighing me down anyway." Ever since they appeared in sixth grade, I'd felt that my breasts didn't belong to me, like they were placed on me by mistake. When girls expressed their jealousy, I found myself wildly perplexed. And likewise when I caught boys staring during class with their tongues practically hanging out, thinking I wouldn't notice. Back then, the entire boob phenomenon went right over my head; I couldn't figure out what everyone was making such a fuss about. But maybe that's because I had really good ones. I didn't long for or lust after them because as far as tits went, I was rich. Is that what it feels like to be born into wealth? Everybody clamors for what you have but you just sit back, super bored in your in-home theater, and think, *So what?*

"Oh my God, that's perfect. We'll go to Dr. Silver first thing in the morning. He'll lop those babies right off and sew them onto me and then—well, what of mine do you want?"

"Uhh . . . ?"

"On my body or my face. If you're giving me your boobs I want to give you something."

"Um, okay, then I want . . ." She rotated so that her legs stayed on the lounge chair while her torso faced me completely, presenting. I studied her face, her opalescent fiber-optic eyes that, though mostly green, seemed to contain flashes of every color. Her perfectly sloped nose, her small mouth with those chubby lips . . . "I want your lips."

"Ah, I do have killer lips, good call. They're not a hundred percent authentic, but they're nice. Everything Dr. Silver does is nice."

"Your plastic surgeon, I'm guessing?"

"I'm one of the only people he still sees, actually," she said, half matter-of-fact, half proud. "He used to do surgery for girls in the eighties. Big-shot plastic surgeon, he did everyone's faces back then. Every actress from like '81 to '99 who got work done, got it done by Dr. Silver. You ever hear the term *silver lips*?"

"Sure," I said, though I hadn't.

"Those big juicy Dominique Le Bon–style lips that suddenly everyone had around that time? They were all done by Dr. Silver. Hence, silver lips."

"Then I'm an admirer of his work," I said, which seemed to please her.

"He retired in 2012 but he's been a darling about making time for me here and there. He's the only one I trust not to fuck up my mouth."

"That's quite the responsibility."

"It's not like I'm a plastic surgery nut, by the way," she added. "I'm not like your Heidi Montags or your Lara Flynn Boyles, I just like getting my lips touched up every now and then. It's collagen injections so you have to get them redone every few months, otherwise they sort of deflate."

"You don't have to explain," I said. "Even if you were more plastic than human I wouldn't be one to judge."

"Rob *hated* them." She rolled her eyes in utter disgust. "That's my ex. He hated my lips and my nail extensions and the dark makeup that I abso-fucking-lutely adore. He said it was *witchy*, like, as if that's a bad thing. Just one of the many reasons I had to dump him." *She* dumped *him*. I knew those Walgreens girls hadn't known what they were talking about. He would have had to be crazy to leave her for another girl, wasn't that obvious?

"I'm sorry, I know breakups aren't—"

"Yeah, but I'm over it." She beamed then, shivering the thought of him off her shoulders. "So we'll call Dr. Silver first thing in the morning and he'll take your boobs and put them onto me and take my lips and put them onto you. I think it'll be a fair trade."

"Oh yes, definitely. Very fair. And very sane."

"Like a friendship necklace, only . . . surgical."

We locked eyes in a moment of quiet, then burst out laughing; the sound broke and scattered in echoes, getting caught and tangled in the trees.

"A friendship necklace," she said again, holding on to the ruby amulet around her neck. "I like that idea. Here." She reached her hands around to unclasp the slender gold chain.

"Oh no," I tried to protest as she moved from her lounge chair onto mine, so there was only a sliver of night between us, "I couldn't."

"But you have to!" she sang. "I insist."

I nodded, more than happy to acquiesce. She draped the amulet over my heart and leaned in to clasp the chain behind my neck. We were eye to eye for that quick moment of understanding, then her lips were pressing onto mine, cool from the night air, plump and hungry and tasting of champagne. Silver lips. For the first time in my life I felt like a very important person.

"There you are!" Olivia whined. She had climbed up onto the roof and was pulling the ribbed black fabric of her dress down over her knees. "We've been looking everywhere for you."

"How long have we been up here, Justine?" Eva-Kate asked me instead of addressing Olivia. "Ten, maybe fifteen minutes?"

"Sure," I said. It could have been ten minutes, it could have been ten hours, I had no idea.

"So then how could they have possibly looked 'everywhere' for me?"

"Everywhere in your ugly house, fuckface." Olivia

scowled at her with impeccable cat eyes. Olivia was very catlike, I realized then, and it wasn't just the eye makeup. Her skinny body moved like it was on the prowl, graceful and easy yet ready to pounce.

"A term of endearment," Eva-Kate assured me.

"Oh, hey." London climbed up behind Olivia. "You found your dog!"

"Yes, yes," Eva-Kate said before I had a second to reply. "Justine found her dog and you've found me. Now tell me, is there a good reason you're interrupting an important conversation with my new neighbor?"

"Josie said to come up here and make sure you weren't doing anything you'd regret," London reported, crossing her arms, sass and affectation levels spiking way off the charts.

"She also said to not say it like that." Olivia glared at her friend. "I think she just wanted us to make sure you're okay."

"I love that psycho bitch, she knows me too well. However, I *did* tell her she only needed to make sure I didn't do anything I'd regret when there were cameras around. So congratulations, you two, your work here is done."

FLASH!

As if on cue, a flash went off from behind London and Olivia, momentarily blinding me.

"Say cheese, bitches." A voice spoke from within the

flash. When I'd blinked enough times to regain my vision, I saw that it was a man in bright though bedraggled clothing, who looked too old to be spending time with high school–aged girls.

"Great timing." Eva-Kate's sarcasm was lazy and noncommittal. "I was just relishing the rare pleasure of not having any cameras around."

"Yeah, well, those precious moments are long gone now, Queenie," he said, pointing the camera at her again. "Your boy Flashbulb is here now."

"*Flashbulb?*" Olivia snickered.

"It's a name he's trying out." London stroked his arm. "It needs some work."

"Um, try *a lot* of work," Olivia teased.

"I kind of like it, to be honest," Eva-Kate said to no one in particular. "It works for him. He's not exactly a class act."

"Hey!"

"It's not an insult," she assured him. "You're a club rat, you're *king* club rat. You own it and you should keep owning it."

From the look of him, she knew what she was talking about. He wore an acid-washed denim vest over a pink tie-dyed V-neck exposing a triangle of patchy chest hair, and a pair of ugly yellow sweatpants. Not that there is such a thing as good-looking yellow sweatpants, but this was a particularly nauseating shade. His white Nikes didn't have laces and he wasn't wearing socks.

"I sure *will* keep owning it," he said, noticing me sitting quietly in Eva-Kate's shadow. "Who's this?"

"Spencer, this is Justine Childs. Justine, this is Spencer Sawyer." Eva-Kate rattled off an introduction, then pointed an accusatory finger at him. "You *cannot* hit on her, Spencer, especially not in front of your girlfriend."

Spencer Sawyer. Photographer and curator of I Know What You Did Last Night. On one hand I was ecstatic, knowing that just by being in his presence I could end up featured on the website, a place I thought I'd only visit in my dreams. On the other hand, I couldn't believe a character so prominent in the LA party scene looked the way he did. I'm not exaggerating when I say he could have been a crackhead wandering in off the streets.

"I'm not his girlfriend." London leaned her head on his shoulder. "We're just friends." The interesting thing about London was that she was the only one of the group who looked like she ate actual food. She was undeniably the shapeliest of them all, and she stood prouder than the others, as if her body was her greatest possession.

"Yeah, friends with benefits," Spencer added. "And I mean *all* the benefits."

"Please do not say 'friends with benefits.'" Eva-Kate looked like she could throw up. "This isn't middle school. If you have to talk like that, do it off my property."

"Queenie is being so queenie tonight," Spencer said to London. "Don't you think?"

"Okay, you." Eva-Kate pointed her finger back at Spencer. "I hope you realize my very dear friend here is way out of your league and if you fuck this up you will be lonely and sexless for a long time."

"Not really," he said, snapping a picture of London as she twisted her silky red hair into a top bun. "I'm Spencer Sawyer; girls will do anything if they think it might get them on IKWYDLN. They'll sleep with guys a lot uglier than me for a lot less, let me tell ya."

"Don't bother." Eva-Kate yawned. "I just realized I don't care."

"Who's thirsty?" Josie climbed up onto the roof with a bucket tucked under her arm. She set the bucket down, revealing that it was filled with ice and clear bottles holding something pink and fizzy.

"Thank God," Eva-Kate groaned. "Josie, as always, you read my mind."

Josie handed her a bottle and Eva-Kate took the top off, casually using her teeth.

"Anyone have a bottle opener for those of us who aren't on Eva-Kate's level of savageness?" Olivia asked. Spencer slid a pair of Wayfarers out of his pocket and showed her how the arms were designed to double as bottle openers. She was impressed.

"Justine, don't you want one?" Eva-Kate took the bottle away from her mouth, exposing newly rosy lips.

"Uhh . . ." I knew I wasn't supposed to mix alcohol

with my medication, but I wondered how much of an impact one drink could realistically have. "What is it?"

"It's called Reign." Eva-Kate held one out to me. "It's my absolute favorite."

"But what is it, like, what's in it?" I took the bottle from her and liked how its neck felt in my hand.

"It's the same thing as an Irish redhead," Olivia explained. "But in a pretty bottle."

I didn't know what was in an Irish redhead, but everyone was staring at me and I didn't want to make myself seem more out of touch than I already had.

"I'll open it for you!" London ripped the bottle from my hand and popped it open using what was evidently her new favorite toy, then handed it back to me. Bubbles fizzed up from the mouth.

"Thank you," I said, then took a deep breath and followed it with my first drink. To my surprise, I loved the taste. The harsh burn of alcohol was buried beneath many layers of bubbly sweetness: a divine concoction of citrus and cherry and mint, not unlike a Shirley Temple.

"Isn't it the best?" Eva-Kate asked, going off my smile.

"Amazing," I said as the delicious taste became a delicious feeling.

"I wanna get in the water," Eva-Kate said, walking to the edge of the roof, looking down onto the pool and the people who still frolicked loudly in it. Somehow since last time I'd seen them they'd acquired two inflatable inner tubes, one a long-necked swan and the other a sprinkled doughnut.

"Let's do it," said London, pulling her black dress off over her head so that she was standing there in nothing but gray Calvin Klein underwear.

"Love the enthusiasm, Lo." Eva-Kate tapped a finger against her lips. "But I'm not in the mood for all those randos."

"You mean your *guests*?" Spencer snapped a picture of us all as we looked down from our pedestal on the roof.

"Are they really my guests if I didn't invite them?"

"If you didn't invite them, then how'd they get in?" London asked, shivering a little.

"Yeah, Eva-Kate," Josie teased. "How'd that happen?"

"Okay, fine, Josie, you were right. Happy?"

"Happy about what?" I asked, speaking out of turn without thinking twice.

"I was trying to be a normal person for once and not have a doorman or bouncers work the party. That's how the randos got in."

"I told her it was a bad idea," Josie boasted.

"Well, excuse me for wanting to not live like a celebrity all the fucking time."

"You're lucky the worst thing that happened was a few unwanted guests. Could have gotten a lot uglier."

"Thanks for the lecture, Mom."

"It's your house, you can tell them to leave. Or better idea, actually, I'll go down and tell them."

"That's true." Eva-Kate thought about it. "That is very true. I'll take care of it." She walked to the corner of the roof and bent down to open a wooden storage unit, then pulled out a dusty megaphone and brought it back with her.

"What are you do—"

"Listen up, everybody!" The megaphone made a high-pitched squeak as she turned it on. "Time to go home. Party's over, fam."

Josie winced.

"Oh boy," she said. "By midnight this will be viral."

The crowd looked up, confused, then looked to each other, then collectively shrugged and resumed whatever it was they'd been doing.

"What the hell?" Eva-Kate looked to Josie. "What's wrong with them?"

"Tell them you're gonna call the cops," Olivia suggested.

"No, no," Josie pleaded. "Remember what we said about not making a scene? Just . . . just . . ."

"Just what?"

"Be polite, okay?"

"Hey, bitches!" Eva-Kate turned the mic back on and screamed into it again. "The cops are on their way. *Please* leave before this gets difficult." She looked back to wink at Josie. "*Thank you*."

This time they got the message, scattering like marbles in every direction.

"Works every time," Olivia deadpanned. "Everybody hates the cops."

"Tomorrow when she's sober she's gonna see herself on YouTube or TMZ, probably both, and scold me for not stopping her," Josie told me. "I have you as my witness that I tried my best."

"To the pool!" Eva-Kate sang out, shooting one arm into the air. Immediately I forgot whatever it was Josie had said. I was too distracted by the way Eva-Kate looked like the Statue of Liberty with her arm up, bottle in hand like a torch, and the fact that I already couldn't remember my life before her.

CHAPTER 10

WHIPLASH GIRL CHILD

I felt nauseous in the back seat of Eva-Kate Kelly's custom periwinkle Audi S7, but I didn't care. I was squished up against the window next to Josie, who pulled her bony shoulders inward as if to avoid touching me. Next to her were London and Olivia, both embracing their hangovers with big bug-eyed glasses and floppy wide-brimmed hats. Princess Leia rode shotgun, Eva-Kate had insisted on it. An unopened package of Red Vines poked out from under the driver seat.

It was nine in the morning and we hadn't slept yet. Time had flown by, reclining by the pool, soaking up the stories they told, watching them like a movie, feeling more awake than I'd ever felt before. I drank Reign until I felt brave enough to get in the water and curl up comfortably into the inflatable swan, carelessly making faces for Spencer's camera. I bobbed up and down with the water, going with the flow. I was in the swim. At sunrise we wrapped ourselves in towels and Eva-Kate ordered an assortment of pastries, which we ate by the fireplace while she told us about the time she went on a date with Robert Pattinson. Spencer said he didn't believe her, so Josie got out the tabloid pictures, and Eva-Kate said, "See? I wasn't lying. I can't have you going around telling people I'm a liar." But I didn't care if her stories were real or not, I loved listening either way.

Have you ever felt that what was happening to you was just too good to be true? That there was no way reality could be giving you exactly what you wanted, that it had to be a dream? A rule of thumb, something I've learned, is that when something seems too good to be true, it is.

"Eva-Kate," London groaned, pressing her palm against the window, "this car wasn't designed for four people back here."

"So?" Eva-Kate shot back, making a right on a red light where a sign clearly warned that this shouldn't be done. She was playing with the radio but wouldn't pick a station, she just scrolled through them so that all we got were staticky snippets of songs spliced together.

"We're squished," said Olivia.

"Oh, you're fine," said Eva-Kate, fiddling with the dial. "Together you skinny bitches weigh a total of, what, a hundred pounds? Plus, we'll be there in a second."

She barreled down the Pacific Coast Highway with her left arm dangling out the window. She took us zigzagging wildly in and out of lanes, sometimes veering into two lanes at once, always followed by a disgruntled blare of a horn, always slamming on her brakes at the last possible second.

"You're gonna get us killed," London complained lazily, like she didn't care one way or the other. I didn't care either. I figured dying in a car crash with Eva-Kate Kelly at the wheel would be the best possible way I could die. A death like that would make the news. A death like that would be remembered, go down in history. That death would not be in vain.

"Don't you think if you're gonna be driving like a fucking lunatic you should get a less conspicuous car?"

"Okay, yes, here it is," Eva-Kate said, finally landing on a station. "I knew I'd find it."

"Rob's new song?" London made a face. "Ew, I hate it already."

Rob Donovan's voice oozed from the speakers, soulful and melodic, accompanied by a catchy collision of strums and drum machine, a whirlpool of synthesized sounds I couldn't exactly identify. Eva-Kate instructed us to be quiet as the song played. It went like this:

When I met you we were young and wild
I liked your soul, you liked my style
I used to stay awake just to hear your voice
Hanging on to every word like I didn't have a
    choice.
Now you say you've had enough, that I just
    make you tired
But I'm gonna have to call your bluff, 'cause
    baby you're a liar

Every night you're in my dreams I can't pretend
    you're not
I liked your cries, you liked my screams, or at
    least that's what I thought
What can I do except pick up the phone and
    call
Only to hear that empty ringing, or hear
    nothing much at all?
Days like this I wish we'd catch some rain
I could wash these memories from me and
    watch them swirling down the drain.

Then the chorus came, and repeated itself three times:

Look at you standing there
You smile at me and you taunt
You know what I need

You know what I want
Meet me in the hotel lobby
At the Chateau Marmont.

"Wonder who it's about," said London.

"It's about me, obviously. We were definitely still together when he wrote it, who else would it be about?" Eva-Kate asked rhetorically.

"Dunno." London shrugged. "Anyone. Or maybe no one."

"He thinks he's a real artist now." I could see Eva-Kate rolling her eyes in the rearview mirror. "It is the most pathetic thing I've ever heard. *Chateau fucking Marmont?* Yeah, real artsy, congrats on being such an innovator."

"Dear Lord," Josie said. "You guys should have heard him talking about how he has a responsibility as a public figure to talk about what really matters instead of putting out more catchy hits like everyone else is." She sounded just as invested in the Rob-as-a-pathetic-relic-of-our-past as Eva-Kate was. "Does he not get that that's literally what pop stars do? It's not his job to be political, it's his job to write fucking catchy hits."

"Oh, as if he writes his songs," said Eva-Kate. "Unless by songwriting you mean jotting down notes and handing it to an actual songwriter."

I didn't like the song. In an attempt to be experimental

it was clunky and disjointed sounding. It conjured images of gulls butting heads and falling into the sea. But that didn't matter—it was a Rob Donovan song and therefore, at this point, a guaranteed hit. Whether it wanted to be or not.

"He's always wanted to be a rock star," said Olivia, "but he's just not."

"Lol," said Eva-Kate. "Hashtag that awkward moment when you think you're a rock star but you're actually just a more famous version of Aaron Carter."

"Who's Aaron Carter?" asked London.

"Seriously?" Eva-Kate was annoyed. "You don't remember Aaron Carter?"

"I don't either," Olivia admitted.

"Ummmm, *Nick Carter's* little brother?"

"Okay, who the fuck is Nick Carter?" London giggled.

"From the Backstreet Boys," Josie condescended. "You can't pretend to be too cool to know who the Backstreet Boys are."

"I mostly grew up internation—" Olivia began, but was cut short by Josie.

"We know, Liv, you mention it at least once a week, and this time it won't help you look cool and mysterious because, guess what, the Backstreet Boys were international celebrities and you know it."

"Saying you don't know who the Backstreet Boys are

is basically just admitting to being a liar," Eva-Kate agreed, clearly proud of her new adage.

"Whatever," Olivia said, and seemed to really mean it. "Justine, you'll have to excuse these two, they romanticize the year 2000 so much you'd think it was the twenties."

"It's true." Eva-Kate wasn't ashamed of this. "I'd say every year between 1995 and 2005. I have a crush on just about every song and every trend from those years."

That explained the clear plastic phone and answering machine pulled straight out of *Nickelodeon Magazine*.

"Ugg boots and Juicy and tattoo chokers and those clunky chain-link bracelets from Tiffany's," Josie recited. "Nobody realized how tacky they were being."

"'All My Life' by K-Ci and JoJo," Eva-Kate wistfully recalled. "'Sex and Candy' by Marcy Playground."

"Hey, what happened to Marcy Playground?" Josie asked.

"You weren't even alive until 2000," Olivia reality-checked. "And there's no way you remember pop culture from when you were five years old."

"*Obviously*," Eva-Kate said. "That's why we can romanticize it, because we weren't around to see how it sucked. Just like you weren't alive during Prohibition even though you act like you were."

"Maybe I was," Olivia challenged her. "In another lifetime."

"Sure, maybe," Eva-Kate said. "That doesn't mean you can pull off a cloche hat, though, does it?"

"Oh please, and you think you can pull off Juicy fucking Couture?"

"That's entirely different," Eva-Kate calmly insisted. "My Juicy tracksuits are a part of a plan."

"A plan to look like Federline-era Britney?"

"No. Well, *yes*, sure, but that's not the point. The point is to bring back a moment in fashion that people believed beyond a shadow of a doubt was dead and buried for good. Sure, yeah, people still love their Juicy Couture, I'm not doubting that. It's just that the *last* thing people are expecting is for Federline-era Juicy suits to make a comeback; that's what will make it such an impressive feat when I single-handedly bring them back in style. Think of it as corpse resurrection."

"What a strange new way to play God." Olivia feigned intrigue. "Very important work, Eva-Kate."

"Like whoever brought back tattoo necklaces from the nineties," Eva-Kate ignored her and went on. "*That* was cool. Once those were over I thought they were going down in the embarrassing-fashion-choices hall of fame for eternity. Watching them reappear has been like watching the dead brought back to life, I swear."

"Who was responsible for the tattoo necklace revival?" I asked, completely enthralled with her train of thought. As far as I was concerned, her plan to bring back Juicy suits was a work of art.

"That's the thing." She sat up excitedly. "No one knows. Whoever it was didn't make sure people knew it was her. She was probably just some *rando* 'it' girl who thought it would be funny to wear one, and then people followed blindly, as they will with an 'it' girl. But I won't make that mistake, everyone is gonna know that Eva-Kate Kelly brought back Juicy suits."

"Again," Olivia joked, "I have to say that this project is not only important, but also *admirable*. Girls, do you think she'll win first or second place at the Nobel Prize convention?"

There's no such thing as a Nobel Prize convention, you sycophant, I thought. I could feel myself getting defensive, but for no reason at all. Eva-Kate clearly didn't need protecting from anybody, let alone from me. She could hold her own, I knew; she could stand her ground in a 9.5 earthquake.

"They actually made one covered in Swarovski crystals that I've been bidding on," she said, ignoring Olivia completely. "It's up to *twenty-five thousand* right now. The tide is high, but I'm holding on. That thing is gonna be mine."

"I *love* this conversation," said London. "And just FYI, if I had to pick a decade to live in, it would be the sixties so I could fuck JFK. Or wait, would that be the fifties?"

Eva-Kate made a sharp left into a parking lot. Every car there was either black or white or silver and cost over $150,000. Eva-Kate's stood out like a jelly bean. I could tell she was proud of this; watching the pleased sideways smirk creep across her face as she tossed the keys to a valet. Her pastel hair poked out beneath the black velour hood of the Juicy jacket with a diamond-encrusted *J* hanging from the zipper, and some kind of iridescent lotion was rubbed into the exposed skin of her chest bone. Her black-as-night sunglasses balanced precariously on the tip of her nose. *This girl*, I thought, *this girl wants to be noticed.*

This was Soho House Malibu (also known as the Little Beach House), an exclusive club for the mostly rich and somewhat famous. I trailed behind the group into the lobby with Princess Leia in my arms, thinking that I had died and gone to heaven.

"Excuse me, miss?" The hostess approached from behind and tapped me on the shoulder. I had to smile so wide it hurt to pretend she hadn't scared the hell out of me. She wore horn-rimmed glasses, and her chestnut hair was in a suspiciously impeccable top bun. "We only permit service dogs."

Never trust a girl with a flawless top bun, I thought.

"Oh . . . I . . ."

"She's with me," Eva-Kate interjected, extending an arm between me and Top Bun.

"But is she a *service dog*?" Top Bun tried again, the corners of her mouth turning down in a preemptively victorious smirk.

"BB, listen." Eva-Kate slipped her sunglasses onto the top of her head, knocking off the velour Juicy hood so that her hair cascaded out in a mesmerizing swish. "I've never seen you before and I'm here all the time, so I'm guessing that means you're new. Now, I pay a lot of money so that I can feel at home here, and you bugging my friend about her dog is not making me feel very at home. So, if you could drop the snobby shopgirl vibe, that would be great. Unless of course you think it would be easier if I spoke to your manager?"

The girl turned her smirk into a rigid smile, then turned the rigid smile into a gracious smile.

"No need, Miss Kelly." She waved us on. "Enjoy your afternoon."

"We sure will, BB," Eva-Kate said, moving on as if the interaction had never happened. "We sure fucking will."

We walked on a Persian rug down a corridor decorated with vintage advertisements and oil pastel flowers on black paper. I followed Eva-Kate up a black wood staircase pressed against a glass window overlooking the gray ocean stretched out beneath us and into a terra-cotta restaurant.

"Justine, come." Eva-Kate beckoned me. "Sit next to me. You can have the head of the table."

"Me?" I felt my voice catch in my throat. My temples throbbed, I felt uneasy on my feet. I was simultaneously starving and repulsed by the idea of eating.

"Yes, you. I can sit next to any of these morons any time I want. You're the guest of honor." She pulled out the chair at the head of the table and gestured grandly for me to sit in it.

"Yeah, okay."

I walked to the chair, feeling the burn of everyone's eyes on me.

"Guest of honor, wow," Olivia mumbled. "This one's really getting the special treatment, huh?"

"Don't take it personally," Eva-Kate said to me. "Olivia's mean to everybody. You wouldn't think someone so pretty would have such a chip on her shoulder, but she does."

"Love ya too, whore." Olivia stuck her tongue out at Eva-Kate and slid languidly into her chair. The chairs were cream-colored suede on mahogany legs that wobbled on stylistically uneven ceramic floors. Eva-Kate sat so that she was in between me and Josie with London and Olivia across from her. Princess Leia curled up complacently by my feet. Eva-Kate raised her wrist limply into the air, holding out her thumb, pointer, and middle finger to catch the waiter's attention. He hurried over, pouring ice waters for everybody.

"Hello, hello, I'm Dennis, I'll be taking care of you this morning. Can I get you kiddos started with some drinks?" Dennis had surfer-blond hair and vividly white veneers. I couldn't tell how old he was, but guessed thirty trying for twenty-four.

"We're ready to order, actually," Eva-Kate yawned, looking down at the menu that was printed in burgundy onto ivory card stock. "Let's do the lemon ricotta pancakes, three of those, please, two acai bowls, the avocado toast, four sides of bacon, and an Elixir of Life for everyone. Thanks so much." She handed the menu over to him, resting her chin in her hand like an egg.

"And . . ." Dennis looked around the table, trying to make eye contact with the rest of us. "Is that for . . . does anybody want anything else?" London opened a pack of sugar and poured it onto a dish. Olivia examined her naked fingernails.

"We're good," Josie spoke up. "That'll be all."

"All righty then." He jotted the order down on a pad and stuck the pen behind his ear. "I'll go ahead and get those menus out of the way for you."

"I do the ordering," Eva-Kate said to me, leaning in. "It's just sort of my thing. But you'll love this food, trust me. And the elixir is honestly to die for."

"Oh, okay," I said. "Yeah, cool."

"Oh, you're just the cutest." Eva-Kate squeezed my cheek between two fingers. "You guys, isn't she just the cutest?"

"Well, don't *patronize* her," said Olivia. "She's not a doll."

"Can we not talk like she's not sitting right here?" London proposed. "It's creepy. Justine, you're not a doll, are you?"

"Um, no." I cleared my throat. "No."

"I'm so hungover I could fucking die," said London. "Does it have to be so bright in here? Jesus."

"We're literally at the beach," said Olivia. "So yeah, it does have to be bright, ya vampire."

London clacked her teeth together with her lips in a snarl, biting the air in Olivia's direction. Josie rolled her eyes so that only I could see, and checked her matte coral lipstick in a shell-shaped compact mirror. The waiter came back with a tray of elixirs—luminous yellowy liquid in laughably skinny glasses. I watched, intrigued, as he set each one down without making eye contact, and then left discreetly without anybody thanking him. I wanted to thank him, but the words came out so timid and unsure of themselves that I doubt he or anybody else heard them. Olivia watched him out of the corner of her eye. When she was sure he was gone, she pulled a flask from her purse and dexterously poured it into her elixir.

"No need to be so sneaky and conspicuous," said Eva-Kate. "They don't care what we put in our drinks. As long as they didn't serve it to us, they can't get in trouble." She meant *inconspicuous*, but I could see how the two might be easy to mix up. Sort of.

"Better safe than getting thrown out of the House for sneaking booze—I'd rather take a long walk off a short pier."

"Suit yourself." Eva-Kate shrugged.

"You want some, then?" Olivia offered.

"No thanks." Eva-Kate wrinkled her nose. "I had enough last night."

"You sure? It's good whiskey. Johnnie Walker Blue."

"Drinking like that will have you wrinkly by twenty-nine, my dear."

"I'm sixteen," Olivia replied. "I honestly don't give a fuck."

I wondered which of them I was more impressed with in that moment. On one hand, there was the girl so in the moment she couldn't be bothered with the faraway concept of aging, and on the other hand was the realist, the girl who believed her beauty was a gift not to be squandered and took precautions against the inevitable. This was how I saw them then, admirable in their girlish wisdom, keepers of a book on role modeling I would have loved to get my hands on.

Sitting so close to them, I felt that I had to be watching a movie. They lived in soft-light Technicolor, blonds so blond and blues so blue and browns in so many varying shades the mind boggled: amber and coffee and chestnut and beige and sepia and auburn and fawn. Their details, from the confused array of bracelets and paper VIP wristbands to skinny black wings drawn onto the outer corners of their eyes—smudged as they were after a night of partying—were so fine and so crisp, somehow both divinely intentional and radically chaotic at the same time. With their enlarged eyes and exaggerated ranges of motion, it was as if they'd been assembled in a fun-house factory.

Next to them I felt drab and lackluster. I wore my pajamas still, with the slippers Eva-Kate had rummaged up for me. If I hadn't been so tired and in awe, I would have been embarrassed to show up looking like I did. And I'm embarrassed now, in retrospect, cringing at the thought of my frizzy hair pulled into a ponytail and what they must have thought of me then. I must have looked like a charity case, like some loser kid Eva-Kate Kelly was taking under her wing for the sake of adding magnanimity and humanitarianism to her public image. And at the time that's what I too thought it was. There was no way, in my mind, that Eva-Kate Kelly genuinely wanted to be friends with someone as unknown and insignificant as I was.

London and Olivia were comparing bruises from the night before, examining each other's arms like apes at a zoo while Josie held her phone up for Eva-Kate to read from. Eva-Kate read with squinted eyes, nodding periodically for Josie to keep scrolling. I didn't know what was happening, but it didn't matter to me. I was sitting at a table with people I'd dreamed about being near, and I knew at this table we were quietly the center of attention, because as I watched them I could see the rest of the room was watching them too, surreptitiously over the tops of their teacups and sideways behind menus. It made perfect sense to me: the guests of the Little Beach House were rich and undeniably in vogue, but there were things far more alluring than money and high fashion. Like what? Like being young and absolutely careless, having money and fame so early in life that you can't imagine it being any other way, and therefore you have no reason to be anything other than confident. It's like how every morning of our lives we've seen the sun rise, so we've never thought to consider maybe once upon a time it didn't, or that maybe one day it won't.

The girls and women around us had money, but money alone couldn't buy confidence. They were all variations of the same thing. Designer jeans and crepe de chine blouses, glimmering hints of gold on their wrists and ears and necks. Suede fedoras and this month's ballet flats, a generous amount of nude-colored makeup applied to create that natural, no-makeup effect. They wore low-cut shirts and push-up bras, they sat up straight and laughed shyly with chins tucked under. They were fresh faced and well rested. Our table stood out in such stark contrast that it made time stand still. Eva-Kate and her crew were pretty, yes, but bedraggled, unraveling at the seams. They were compact paradoxes: rich vagrants, street urchins living in high castles. And how they were still awake I had no idea. Their eyelids sagged but their bodies moved speedily, exuding energy. It was like nothing I'd ever seen before, and if I hadn't known any better

I would have wondered if they were even human at all, or another species entirely.

"Oh, it's not so bad," Eva-Kate said to Josie once she'd stopped scrolling. "I kept all my clothes on this time, didn't I?"

"Yes." Josie laughed. "Yes, you did."

"Surveying last night's damage?" Olivia asked from across the table.

"Hardly any," Eva-Kate reported. "The *Daily Mail* picked up the story about me shouting from my roof and there are some less-than-flattering pictures on TMZ, but that's pretty much it. Am I getting . . . boring?"

"Not boring," Josie corrected her. "You're just taking my good advice more than you used to."

"Hate it when you're right." Eva-Kate kissed Josie on the cheek. "Okay, moving on. Speaking of pictures, anyone have any good ones from last night?"

"Is the pope Jude Law?" Olivia asked. London giggled but Eva-Kate rolled her eyes.

"I took a bunch," said Josie. "Sending them now."

"What about Spencer?" Eva-Kate asked London. "Where are his pics?"

"I doubt he's even going to be awake for the next six to eight hours," London said.

"True. Well, make sure to text when they're up," Eva-Kate said. Her phone dinged in her lap and she got distracted. "Ooh, Josie, these are dope."

"I like the one of you lounging on your bed with the dog," said Olivia.

"Yes!" Eva-Kate agreed, putting her phone flat on the table so that I could see: It was Eva-Kate reclining like an Egyptian queen with her nose pressed up against Princess Leia's nose. It must have been taken right before I got upstairs and found them. Now Eva-Kate was filtering the photo and uploading it to Instagram.

"What's your Insta?" Eva-Kate asked me, typing out a caption that read: *Surprise guests, Justine and Princess Leia! #poolparty #goldenpuppy #AlwaysDownForNew Friends*

"Me?"

"You, dummy."

"It's, uh, it's . . ." I didn't want to say. I had come up with it three years ago and knew it would sound childish now. Plus all it had on it was my photography—abandoned houses, stripped billboards, and other wannabe artist stuff—and I wasn't ready for Eva-Kate to see that.

"Do you not have an Instagram?" Olivia prodded, irritated. "If you don't have an Instagram just say you don't have an Instagram."

"Be nice," Eva-Kate warned.

"I do have an Instagram." I hurried the words out before the notion that maybe I didn't could spread. "It's Love underscore Song."

"Cute," she said, typing. "Romantic."

"No, actually, it's just a poem by T. S. Eliot. 'The Love Song of J. Alfred Prufrock.' And it's not all that romantic."

"I *know* the poem," she said unconvincingly as my Instagram loaded onto her screen. "I wasn't born yesterday."

With one eye I ambivalently peered at her phone, squeamish that I'd find my Instagram to be more embarrassingly childish than I remembered. There weren't that many pictures posted. Luckily. The two most recent were of Princess Leia curled up on my bed, backdropped by the white-iron, spiraling bed frame. The third one was of elevator buttons lit up green, a piercing hue that had caught my attention as I left the doctor's office on Wilshire. The fourth was of roses beneath a thickly clouded sky, filtered through Amaro and then enhanced. The last one, taken a year and a half ago, was of Bellflower: long fingers of ivy climbing up a wrought iron gate.

"I don't get the bio." She tilted her head from left to right as if this would help her understand it. I didn't have to look to remember that my bio read: *I have measured out my life with Taylor Swift albums.*

"Oh." I blushed. "Right, so, uh . . . in the poem, 'The Love Song of J. Alfred Prufrock,' he says, 'I have measured out my life with coffee spoons' . . . So, it's like that, except with Taylor Swift albums . . ." Eva-Kate looked at me blankly, so I kept talking. "Because, like, her albums are a way to keep track of time and are, like, an easy way to remember when things happened in my life. You know, so, if I'm thinking about a time when . . . let's say a time I went ice skating at the Culver City rink and I want to figure out what year it was, I can say, oh, well, I remember 'You Belong with Me' was playing and it was the first time I'd ever heard it so it had to be 2009, which means I was eight. For example." My face was hot and I was talking too fast. Somewhere in the back of my mind I thought: *If she really did know the poem she would have gotten the reference.*

"Taylor Swift," Eva-Kate repeated, as if the name were the only thing I'd said. "Are you a fan?"

The way she said it, I could tell there was a right answer and a wrong answer, I just didn't know which was which.

"Sometimes," I said, wishing I could have a sip of Reign or be brave enough to ask Olivia for some of her whiskey.

"We're invited to some pool party with her," she said casually, drinking her elixir. "When she's on a break from her tour. I wasn't gonna go but we can if you want."

"Wow." I had to play this right: too excited would come off as desperate, but not excited enough would result in us not going to the party. "I mean, if you're up for it I'd love to go."

"Is it in Rhode Island?" Olivia asked. "Like for Fourth of July?"

"No," said Eva-Kate.

"Why not?"

"How should I know?" Eva-Kate made her voice sound painfully bored. "And why would I care?"

My phone vibrated and two notifications popped up on the screen:

EVAKATEKELLY started following you.
EVAKATEKELLY tagged you in a post.

I opened the Instagram app and saw the photo of Eva-Kate with my dog. Princess Leia looked like a real princess, sitting in a lap of luxury she'd never known. And yes, I know that I was projecting, so no you don't have to point that out. Above, Eva-Kate's bio read:

First class and fancy free.
(Yeah, I'm the girl from that show.)

"Love it," I said, mimicking her language, giving her my most grateful smile.

My phone went off again.

You have sixteen new followers.

My heart skipped a beat. I'd never had more than eleven followers, and they were just Riley, Abbie, Maddie, and some kids I didn't really know that well from school. People who followed me by default.

My phone vibrated again, another notification.

BellaBoo is now following you.

BellaBoo commented on your picture: *WTF how are you friends with Eva-Kate Kelly? I'm too jelly. Hehe, no rhyme intended ;)*

I giggled then, I couldn't help it. I didn't understand how I could have gone from pining voyeur to friends with Eva-Kate Kelly in the span of twenty-four hours. I felt chosen and lucky as hell. I felt that my particles were drifting away from each other, fizzing out and up in a bubbly flurry. I put my hands on my cheeks to make sure I was still in one piece.

"You'll get a ton of followers now," Eva-Kate told me. "So you should probably rebrand."

"What do you mean?"

"Your Insta is fine and all, it just doesn't have personality. Well, it has some. It needs more. You need a brand."

"A brand?"

"Yeah, like who is Justine Childs? What does she stand for, what does she represent?"

"I . . . I really don't know. Maybe—"

"I have an idea," she interrupted, too inspired to contain herself. "You can be Eva-Kate Kelly's edgy, mysterious new friend—kinda dark, kinda weird—who legit doesn't give a fuck and is way smarter than anybody else."

"Uh . . ."

"Just give me your phone," she said. "This will be easy. Trust me."

Hesitantly, I held it out for her and she snatched it up with her glossy, glittery claws. I watched as she uploaded pictures from last night's party onto my Instagram, adding tags upon tags, filters upon filters. She changed my name from Love_Song to Whiplash_Girlchild, then opened my bio and added to it so that it said: *I have measured out my life with Taylor Swift albums. / May or may not be a nightmare dressed like a daydream.*

"There." She handed the phone back to me. "Now you'll be remembered."

"Thanks . . . but why?"

"Because now you're a character, a persona. Or at least you're on your way to being one. People are stupid, their brains don't hold on to information unless it's broken down in very simple, digestible pieces. We'll change your profile pic later, it should be of your face, not some . . . plant, or whatever that is. Actually, why don't you go to the bathroom and take some selfies in the mirror, Little Beach House mirror in the background of a profile pic will do a lot for you. You'd be surprised."

I believed her. I thought to ask where the bathroom was, but decided I'd come off much breezier and in-the-know if I headed away from the table confidently.

✼ ✼ ✼

I turned the faucet on and let hot water wash over my hands. It was a relief to be alone for a moment. I snapped some pictures of myself looking into the brass-rimmed mirror, but my eyes had circles under them and my hair was a frizzy mess. I took my hair down, brushed it with my fingers, then twisted it into a high bun, hoping I'd look more presentable this way. I took my sweater off and threw it in the trash bin. In plaid PJ bottoms and a blue, thinning shirt from Old Navy, no bra, I almost looked like I could be one of them, the shabby to their shabby chic. I took two or three more pictures, twisting my torso and folding my arms to find my better sides and angles, then decided it was hopeless and glowered at myself. I saw myself in a new context then. I was no longer just myself. Now I was myself compared to Eva-Kate and her friends, myself compared to the other girls and women dining at the surrounding tables. The whole thing was unnerving.

I swung the bathroom door open and was going to head back to the table, but stopped when I saw Eva-Kate down the hall talking to our waiter. I didn't want to interrupt, but I also didn't want to walk past without saying anything, and I couldn't think of any other way out of this besides staying right where I was, so I stood pressed flat up against the wall, figuring they'd be less likely to see me in the mood lighting. I had the fact that neither of them were facing me working in my favor.

"You are hilarious, Dennis," I could hear Eva-Kate say. She laughed, touching his arm.

"Oh . . ." He laughed back. "Well, glad someone thinks so."

"Hey, so, where's Liza? Is she working today?"

"Liza?"

"Liza McKelvoy." Liza McKelvoy. I'd heard the name before. It was those girls at Walgreens, they'd said that Rob broke up with Eva-Kate for Liza McKelvoy. That Eva-Kate must hate it.

"No, I know who you meant, obviously. It's just, she doesn't work here anymore. She hasn't worked here in months, didn't you know that?"

"Oh, right." Eva-Kate shook it off. "I must have forgot. She's always hopping from place to place."

"Guess so, yeah."

"Where's she working now? I'm sure she told me, I just get all these places mixed up, you know?"

"Sure, sure." I could tell he was putting in extra effort to be friendly and was getting impatient. "Last I heard she was bartending at Chateau Marmont. I'm surprised you haven't—"

"*Chateau Marmont?*" From where I stood I could see her entire body lock into place. When she stood still, so did the world around her.

"Yes . . . ," Dennis confirmed nervously. "Is that . . . bad?"

"No, no." Eva-Kate regained her composure, calmly tucked her hair behind her ears. "I just wasn't sure I heard you right. Chateau . . . *Marmont*?" She was a great actress, I realized in that moment. She went from paralyzed to casually addled in the blink of an eye, and very convincingly.

"Exactly," he said, relieved, believing he'd misread her confusion as anger. "It's a lovely hotel, highly recommend it."

"Oh, is that so? Well, then." She was slipping out of character again, sarcasm wiggling its way into her words like a snake. I could see her balling her hands into two fists.

"I should get back to my tables." Dennis untucked a notebook from his apron. "Great chatting, Eva-Kate." He slipped past her and back out into the light of the beachfront restaurant. When she saw that he was gone, she dug her fingernails into her scalp and let her head hang.

"*Chateau Marmont*, are you fucking kidding me?" she muttered under her breath.

I knew what she must have been thinking: If Rob's new song was called "Chateau Marmont" and now it turned out Liza had been working at Chateau Marmont, then the song wasn't about Eva-Kate after all. It was about Liza. *Eva-Kate must hate that. She must be losing her mind.*

None of this made sense to me. I didn't understand why Rob would break up with Eva-Kate *at all*, let alone for a *waitress. She'd have to be one remarkable waitress*, I thought, and tried to imagine a face more uniquely gorgeous than Eva-Kate's, or a personality more bewitching. It was like trying to imagine what nothingness looks like, what existed before the big bang and what will exist once this is all gone. In other words, it couldn't be done.

CHAPTER 11

SONGS

"*I* have to run an errand," Eva-Kate said to us all as we waited for the valet to bring her car around. "Justine is coming with me. Josie, will you call an Uber for the rest of you, please?"

"You got it." Josie took out her phone.

"Why are you taking *her*?" Olivia objected. "You barely know her."

"Because, unlike you, she's interesting to talk to."

I avoided eye contact with Olivia. Nobody had ever called me interesting before; nobody had ever been interested to hear what I had to say. Enter Eva-Kate.

✷ ✷ ✷

There were dark, tumbling clouds along the road as Eva-Kate drove us south down the 405 with her hand resting on mine, "Venus in Furs" by the Velvet Underground playing from the speakers. For someone so delicate-looking and emotionally aloof, Eva-Kate very much liked to touch and be touched. Even if it was just to have someone's hand against her hand, as mine was now. In the short time I'd known her, I'd often see her spontaneously interlace her fingers with whomever she was talking to, or nuzzle her head into the crook of someone's lucky, unsuspecting neck, like a kitten. She could touch whomever she wanted, whenever she wanted, because there wasn't a person around who wouldn't be delighted and honored by her body making contact with theirs.

"So, as you know, I dated Rob for a few years," she said, breaking the silence. "We were always breaking up and getting back together, you know how teenagers can be." She said this nostalgically, as if her teenage years were far behind her.

"Of course," I said, though I'd only ever seen that dynamic on TV—*Friends*, *One Tree Hill*—and in the 2012 Taylor Swift hit "We Are Never Ever Getting Back Together."

I wondered, from time to time, which of two ways this lyric was intended. Was it A: you can go talk to your friends, or talk to my friends, or even talk to me, but we're never getting back together, or was it B: you can go talk to your friends about it, who will tell my friends about it, who will tell me, but still, we're never getting back together? When I'd asked Riley which one she thought it was, she'd looked concerned and said, "I think you're overanalyzing it, Justine. It's just a stupid pop song." I didn't really mind, I knew she was wrong.

"A lot of people thought the whole thing was for publicity, but it wasn't," Eva-Kate went on then. "We were really in love." She picked up a bag of Red Vines and ripped it open with her teeth. "We fought all the time but we were the real deal. At the end of the day we could only trust each other. We had other people in our lives, yes, sure, but in our minds it was us against the world. If we had it our way, we would have been alone, just the two of us; no distractions, no interruptions."

"That sounds really nice," I said, thinking, *I want something like that. I'm tired of being up against the world by myself, I want someone to be on my team.*

"It was. And now it's over."

"You broke up with him."

"Nope. That's just what I want people to think."

Wait, *what*? Why was she telling me this?

"Then . . . what happened?"

"He fell in love with . . . someone else. And I just found out she works at Chateau Marmont, which means his new song is about her. *Not me.* It's humiliating, Justine, I can barely handle it."

"I'm really sorry, Eva-Kate."

"Thank you, but you don't have to be. I'm gonna be fine, I just need some help healing. That's where we're going now, to see Ruby Jones, crystal healer, astrologist, Wiccan extraordinaire. She'll fix me right up."

The entire coast between Los Angeles and San Diego is lousy with beach towns, but about halfway down there is one that stands out among the rest. It stands out for its massive modern Spanish Colonial Revival estates and lazurite-blue pools visible from airplanes, and toxic sunsets, pink and purple, blotchy and dappled, like how you might imagine bruises would appear on a Barbie Doll. This was San Onofre, an opulent offshoot of Orange County, more resort than it was town, where the wealthy and dull went to retreat from the world into their multimillion-dollar fortresses, never to be seen again. I couldn't tell you the actual demographic of San Onofre, because there's never anybody on the streets. They hide out, air-conditioned and insulated, oblivious and impervious to the planet's many states of disarray.

But San Onofre isn't actually known for any of these things. It's known for what you see when you drive past it on the freeway: the San Onofre nuclear power plant. Two domes, each one a hundred and fifty feet high with a thimble-shaped antenna fixed on top, and a blinking cherry-red light on top of that, leaking into the surrounding mist. The domes are completely, symmetrically round like two swollen fruits, so plump and stiff and juicy, so ripe they could burst open at any moment, so ripe they could be on the verge of rot.

"Songs," Eva-Kate said, gazing out the window as we pulled onto Old Pacific Highway, a dusty strip of cracked cement where the freeway shriveled up and ended, over which the two domes loomed.

"*Songs?*" I asked, assuming she'd mumbled and I'd misheard.

"SONGS," she repeated. "San Onofre Nuclear Generating Station. SONGS." She said it with a hint of pride, pleased with herself for knowing this acronym. It was endearing, like a schoolgirl in a spelling bee.

"I see," I said, though that didn't explain much or answer any of my questions, such as why we were driving, at eleven in the morning, toward these bloated monstrosities.

"They're pretty controversial," she said, turning back to them. "They store more than four thousand tons of radioactive waste. They're old and unreliable, sitting right near an earthquake fault line, completely vulnerable to tsunamis. And with millions of people living nearby. Experts say it's a disaster waiting to happen."

"Why don't they just shut them down?"

"Some people are trying. Activists, politicians. But you can't just take them down and make it all go away. I mean, where would all that nuclear waste go?"

"Right," I said, knowing absolutely nothing about

what she was saying, a shadow of trepidation expanding in my gut, fluttering. "So then . . . what are we doing here?"

"Oh, we're not doing anything here. This is just how we get to where we're going."

We drove past the reactor and onto Chaisson Drive. It was a short street with a dead end of grassy bluffs. We stopped in front of the least noticeable house on the block, flat roofed and only one story high, hidden in the shadows of the arrogant Spanish Colonials. Parked in the driveway was an old decommissioned police car, gloss sanded down to matte, the back two windows fogged up with spray paint.

"What do you want to do with Princess Leia? We won't be too long," Eva-Kate said. "No more than an hour."

An hour? I hadn't slept in twenty-six and was beginning to wonder if I'd be able to keep my eyes open for another ten minutes, let alone another hour. But I'd do it, I told myself, I'd stay awake as long as my lucidity was needed.

"She'll be fine in the car," I said. "Just leave the window cracked."

Eva-Kate knocked on the door, splintering and seafoam-painted. I shivered, goose bumps spreading over my bare arms. The air seemed to have dropped at least ten degrees, and wind just slightly too strong to be called a breeze battered the palm fronds, making them hiss and rattle. The door opened and there stood a boy, tall and lanky, about fifteen or sixteen, wearing only jeans and a turquoise pendant on a chain around his neck. His upper chest and arms were covered in black ink tattoos, making him look like he could be older, but the baby fat in his cheeks gave him away.

"E-K-K." He grinned lazily, revealing a dollar sign on his right canine tooth. "Long time."

"Declan, this is Justine. Justine, Declan."

"Hi," I said, keeping my eyes focused diagonally upward, hoping this would come off as blasé.

"She can't come in here," he said to Eva-Kate without acknowledging me. "You know that."

"I already texted Ruby, she gave the thumbs-up." Eva-Kate pulled out her phone to show him the text. He squinted at it, tilting his head sideways.

"Well, whaddya know?" he said, pulling the door back for us to pass through. "Right this way, ladies."

The house was lit with black-shaded floor lamps, no overhead light whatsoever, and smelled strongly of incense and sandalwood oil, wafting in and out with the ocean breeze. He took us through the mostly empty living room and into a low-ceilinged, low-lit hallway, which led to a dark wood door covered from top to bottom in illegible, indecipherable carvings.

"Knock, knock." Declan spoke into the door. "I have Eva-Kate Kelly. And she has a guest with her."

"Well?" called a voice from the other side. "What are you waiting for? Let them in."

Declan rolled his eyes and used a key to unlock the door, then pushed it open.

On a cluster of velvet pillows and cushions beneath a silky white canopy sat a girl applying black nail polish to her toes. She had big curlicue hair and long, twiggy limbs, skin tan and smooth as a polished stone. She wore a threadbare nightgown that hardly covered her thighs; she seemed completely unbothered by, even unaware of, the bite in the air. Sitting on the floor to either side of her were two boys, topless and scrawny like Declan, also with tattoos. Both looked tired; neither seemed to have anything to do. I saw them and quickly averted my eyes, embarrassed but not sure for who. When the girl saw us standing there, she pushed the polish bottle aside and sprang to her feet.

"Eva-Kate, light of my life!" she gushed, pulling Eva-Kate in for a hug. "It's been too long."

"My love, I know," Eva-Kate said, kissing the girl on her mouth, plush and velvety as the cushions on the floor. "I don't know why you have to live so far."

"You know I can't handle LA." The girl grimaced. "Too many vampires. Everybody wants to suck your soul. I'd like to hang on to mine."

"You're not wrong," Eva-Kate agreed, still holding on to the girl's long, bejeweled fingers, still keeping eye contact. "And I wouldn't want anything to happen to your precious soul."

I'd yet to see Eva-Kate so attentive. She looked up at the girl with the respect you'd give to a wise elder or an accomplished leader, though from what I saw, the girl couldn't be much older than Eva-Kate, if even at all. I flinched with a small pang of envy.

"And who's this?" the girl asked, turning to me.

"My neighbor, Justine. You can trust her, she's one of us."

"I know you'd never bring someone who wasn't," she said to Eva-Kate, though she kept her eyes pinned to mine. "I'm Ruby." She extended her hand to me.

"Nice to meet you," I said, taking her hand, an odd combination of extreme temperatures; her skin radiated heat while the dozens of silver rings were cold as ice. Face-to-face I saw that though her skin was baby soft, her eyes were deep set and disarming, so dark brown they were almost black, with hints of green and gold freckled throughout. And they were old eyes, eyes that had seen and been seen, eyes that knew things I'd never know. Even Eva-Kate's relentlessly moony glow was quenched in her presence. She tilted her head from side to side as if examining me. I wondered what Eva-Kate had meant by "she's one of us."

"Come relax," Ruby said. "You must need it after the long drive."

Eva-Kate tensed and stiffened. I tried to decipher her tension. Did I detect a hint of trepidation? Could it be possible she was afraid?

"Oh, okay, sure," she said, squeezing my hand. "Come on, Justine, let's sit."

The boys on the floor made room for us, parting so we could step onto the cushions. They'd been so quiet and still I had forgotten they were there. They kept their eyes to the ground. One, I saw, was turning a bright blue stone over and over in his hand.

Ruby pulled a pack of American Spirits out from under a cushion, put one between her lips, and lit it. Inhaled. She didn't offer one to either of us, which I was grateful for.

"Let's get to it, shall we?" she said.

"Sure." Eva-Kate smiled. "Whatever you want."

Ruby stood up and walked to a bronze-painted dresser and opened a top drawer, retrieving a bundle of cloth. She held it carefully in cupped hands, bringing it back to us like a swaddled baby. She pulled back the fabric piece by piece, revealing two bulbous, misshapen crystals, each the size and approximate shape of a human fist.

"These are very powerful," Ruby said. "I brought them back from Brazil just five days ago. You have to be careful with them."

"Of course." Eva-Kate nodded dutifully.

"This one is rose quartz." Ruby placed her palm over

a pink one. "It will attract love like a magnet attracts metal; keep it in your purse wherever you go, wash it with salt water at night. Sleep with it by your side always."

"It's gorgeous," Eva-Kate said, awestruck.

"This one is museum-grade moldavite." She moved her palm to the second one, mossy green and translucent as glass. "It's extremely rare. There are only fifty-five thousand pounds of it in existence, scattered around the planet. That's basically the size of a Greyhound bus. So if you imagine it spread out across the world, you'll realize just how little of it there actually is. Hundreds of years ago a meteorite fell to Earth and landed in Czech Republic, and in 1786 scientists discovered that it brought these crystalline formations with it. They called these formations moldavite for the town of Moldauthein, where the stones were found."

"Can I touch it?" Eva-Kate asked.

"Of course, it's going to be yours soon. Go ahead."

Eva-Kate touched the clear green surface. A visible shiver rippled up her arm.

"Oh my God." She took her hand away. "What was that?"

"Like I said, this is very powerful and needs to be handled carefully. It's a good sign that it responded to you so strongly. It can do some psychic damage if it doesn't resonate with your energy. But I suspected you were meant to have this stone. Now I know for sure."

It took some effort not to roll my eyes.

"Is moldavite stronger than the others? I mean, I literally felt . . . like . . . little currents running up my arm."

I was dying to know if Eva-Kate really believed in all this, and if so, to what degree?

"Moldavite is the only gemstone that doesn't grow on Earth. It's extraterrestrial debris, coming to us from out there in the universe, carrying with it the power of the cosmos. So, yes, some would say it's the most powerful."

We sat there in silence, the three of us, just staring at the faceted chunk of moldavite. Powerful and sentient or not, it *was* beautiful. I didn't know if I was transfixed or just breaking down from exhaustion, but I couldn't find the will to look away. I was gathering the courage to ask if I could have a turn to touch it when Ruby broke the silence.

"There are so, so many uses for this stone, so many ways to harness and utilize its power, but I'm giving this to you for a few specific purposes. As I've told you before, Eva-Kate, you are one of the Star Children, which has caused you to have a deep feeling of not belonging in this world, a feeling that breeds sadness and hopelessness, and can lead to a chaotic, tumultuous life if not addressed. This moldavite will help you to acclimate to the Earth plane so that you can properly take advantage of all the healing energies it has to offer."

Ruby lit a cluster of sage leaves and twirled it through the air as she spoke.

"Secondly, this precious moldavite will encourage rapid transformation in your life, releasing the toxic things and people that don't serve your highest path. It will give you the clarity you need to sever those ties, and the strength to do so by whatever means necessary. Lastly, when you take a bath holding the moldavite to your chest, it will engage with your heart chakra, returning a tranquil pink glow to your aura, enriching it with the powers of unconditional love. If you do this often enough, anybody who is incapable of giving you unconditional love will magically vanish from your life. Moldavite will harmonize well with the rose quartz, supercharging it to more powerfully attract the right types of love into your life."

"These are exactly what I need." Eva-Kate's jaw practically hung open. "How did you know literally the exact stones I absolutely need in my life right now?"

"It's pretty obvious, my treasure." Ruby stroked the side of Eva-Kate's cheek with the back of her hand. "You came in here sizzling with degraded energies and a murky lemon-yellow aura. Not to mention your normally very orange aura was so fogged up it was practically gray. Don't worry, though, it's better now. And it will keep getting stronger and stronger with the help of these stones."

"Thank God for you, Ruby. You're an actual earth angel." Eva-Kate turned to me. "Justine, wasn't I just saying how she's an earth angel?"

"You were," I said, and smiled at Ruby, though Eva-Kate had not said this or anything like it to me.

"We're *all* earth angels." Ruby laughed breezily, reaching for a roll of bubble wrap propped up against the wall. "Let me wrap these up for you."

"So, then, the price we discussed over text?" Eva-Kate asked, reaching into her purse.

"This moldavite really wants to be with you, so I'll take a hundred off the original price."

"Oh, you don't have to do that," Eva-Kate protested parenthetically, producing a bulky envelope from her purse. "But you're sweet for offering."

She tore open the envelope and began dexterously counting out hundred-dollar bills in a pile on the floor. I quickly lost track of the amount she'd laid down. But the stack had grown tall, that much I knew. She took it in her hands, lining up any wayward bills, then nonchalantly handed it over to Ruby, as if it were not at all unusual to carry thousands in cash. I gawked at her miniature Saint Laurent shoulder bag and couldn't believe so much cash had been tucked away inside this whole time.

"Exquisite," Ruby said, folding the stack in half and binding it to itself with a pin she plucked from her hair. "Was there one more thing you wanted to discuss?"

"Right, yeah." Eva-Kate zipped her purse shut and turned to me. "Could you give us a minute?"

I glanced back and forth between Ruby and Eva-Kate two or three times before it registered that she was talking to me, and a moment after that before I realized she was asking me to leave. My mind reeled with worst-case scenarios: Eva-Kate and Ruby would abandon me here, in San Onofre, with these zombie-eyed boy servants, and I'd be stranded in this reality-adjacent beach house forever, incapable of finding my way home.

"Uh . . ." I turned my neck to look at the door behind me. "Sure, of course. I'll just be in the hall?" I sounded like a doormat and hated myself for it, but the adrenaline high of being chosen as Eva-Kate Kelly's consort on this after-hours outing eclipsed the self-loathing tenfold.

"Zander?" Ruby called out aimlessly. One of the boys who still sat obediently on the floor stood up, keeping his chin slightly tilted down. Out of the two boys he was the dark one, black shaggy hair and heavy-lidded eyes. Standing up, I saw that he wasn't as scrawny as he'd seemed sitting in the shadows, and he was much taller than I'd thought. He towered above Ruby, who had to be at least five ten, and as he stood, defined bundles of muscle shifted beneath the skin of his chest and biceps.

"Take Justine to the kitchen and offer her a drink."

"Yes, Ruby."

"And Eva-Kate, do you want anything? We have virtually any beverage you could ask for."

"I'm good, but thank you." Eva-Kate locked her eyes onto mine and widened them, shifting them left and right as if trying to tell me something. But whatever her message, it was beyond indecipherable.

"Follow me," Zander said, walking ahead to open the door.

"Oh, you know, I'm actually not thirsty, so I'm really fine just—"

"Justine," Eva-Kate said, her voice stern but sweet, as if trying to negotiate with a misbehaving child. "It's totally fine, Zander is the best. Ruby just needs me alone for one second."

"*One* second," Ruby repeated.

I smiled through my nerves and trailed cautiously behind Zander as he walked back down the hallway and through the living room to a cavernous dining area with wooden booths for tables and a rainbow of liquor bottles crookedly lined up on a white porcelain-tiled counter.

"Anything you want," Zander said, opening his palms toward the liquor like a sedated game show host. His palms were calloused and lightly stained the muted, dusty orange-red of bricks. "We got whiskeys, vodkas, rums, gins, tequilas, wines, lagers, liqueurs, and . . . pretty much any mixer you could imagine." He stood with his hip cocked to one side, becoming loose and casual, shaking off the stiff obedience he had worn just a moment ago in Ruby's room.

"Thank you, really, but just a water would be great." I held on to my right wrist with my left hand and let both arms hang down in front of me, a shy attempt at a protective shield. He laughed and narrowed his eyes at me, suspicious, as if I were joking.

"Water?" he sneered playfully. "You do realize standing before you are literally the finest bottles of alcohol in the world, don't you?"

"First of all, I did *not* realize." I adopted his mocking tone of voice, finding that as he relaxed, so could I. "But second of all, I just wouldn't know what to pick."

"*Ohhhh*, okay," he said, like he had just solved a riddle. "I get it. I'll just pour you a glass of what I'm having. You can sit down if you want."

I didn't want to sit down. Sitting down would make the separation from Eva-Kate feel more real. But I also didn't want to stay standing where Zander could keep sneaking glances up and down my body, where I knew I must have looked conspicuously awkward, like a weed in a flower bed. So I sat. Seemingly pleased, he uncorked a translucent olive-green bottle that made me think of the opening scene from *The Rescuers*. Bernard, a mouse, climbs into a green bottle just like that one to retrieve an SOS letter that was written by an orphan named Penny and tossed out to sea. I hadn't seen the movie in a decade, but I vaguely remembered that after the troublesome ordeal of maneuvering his way into the belly of the bottle, he found himself stuck there and couldn't get back out.

Zander poured pale amber liquid from the bottle into two lowball glasses, dropped an oversized ice cube into each one, and set the less-full of the two down in front of me. The single ice cube rattled tenderly against the glass. He sat down across from me and took a velvet pouch from his pocket, letting it flop down onto the table next to his drink.

"Lagavulin 16," he said. "Single-malt scotch aged sixteen years. Should warn you this is strong stuff. I didn't water it down because, well, you seem like you can handle it."

"I do?" I raised an eyebrow.

"I bet you're the kind of girl who looks really dainty and innocent but is secretly tough as rubber. Just remember, the burn is the best part. You gotta savor the burn." He lifted the glass to me and then took a big gulp, wrinkling up his face in an odd mixture of pain and pleasure.

"Ahhhhh," he breathed, mouth wide. "Your turn."

It's just like jumping into cold water, I told myself. *It only hurts for a split second and then you're happy you did it.*

I closed my eyes and braced myself, then took a sip. It was the closest thing to gasoline that I'd ever tasted, and yet I liked it. No, I loved it. The burn was better than he'd promised; it was a rush of stars to the head, a comforting warmth trotting through my veins. A key in a lock. I licked the remainder off my lips and let my eyelids flutter in relief.

"Damn." Zander sat back. "Guess I was right about you. I like to think I can spot a whiskey girl when I see her."

"Guess you can," I said, buzzing.

"But damn," he repeated. "You didn't even flinch."

"It's not that strong." I shrugged, playing to his newly conceived version of me. "I dunno, I just like it." I took another sip, bigger this time, to show how truly unaffected I could be. I drank the entire glass easily, like water, but slowly so that I could savor it, like he'd told me to. The warmth worked its way through my veins, relaxing my muscles that had been clenched and strained for as long as I could remember. I hadn't realized just how tense I had been until the drink started flowing through me. Suddenly I wasn't paralyzed by what Eva-Kate and her friends might think of me, I wasn't haunted by the things Riley had said on the last day of school or what had happened years ago on the set of *Chasen's*, I wasn't angry at my parents or embarrassed about not having money or insecure about my middle-class clothes. The million chatty voices in my head quieted down to a low simmer. It wasn't that I felt confident or beautiful or even bottom-line deserving, it was just that for the first time I didn't have to think about it. After that first glass, nothing could get to me. I had a force field. I felt everything that had ever hurt me melt and drip away off my body into a shower drain from which nothing could return.

"Can't believe I never tried this before," I thought out loud. "I like the way it stings the corners of my mouth where the skin is delicate."

"Nice, right? Want another?"

"That's okay." I rested my chin on one hand and examined the empty glass like an appraiser. "Everything is golden and lovely now, I wouldn't want to mess that up."

"Fair enough." He laughed and took out a pack of Camels. "Can I offer you one or are you just gonna shut me down again?"

"Of course you can," I said, forgetting any reason one could ever have not to smoke a cigarette. "A cigarette sounds nice right about now."

He stuck one in between my lips and lit it, cupping the flame with one hand. We sat back, watching the smoke rise and swirl and eddy in the air, forming clouds on the ceiling with no way out. I didn't let any smoke all the way back into my lungs. If I did, I knew I'd cough and cough until the vessels in my eyes burst, and then Justine, tough girl scotch drinker, would vanish.

He tapped the cigarette against the rim of an ashtray shaped like an empty turtle shell flipped upside down, exposing the white skin of his inner wrist to the light. I saw the hint of a fading tattoo, but I couldn't make out what it was. From where I sat, it looked like a short zigzagging line with an L-shape at the end.

"You know what?" he asked.

"What?"

"You could be hot if you tried."

"Um, fuck you, I'm hot now."

"You're like . . . a five. But if you put some effort in, you could be, I dunno, like a seven or eight. Maybe even a nine."

"*Effort?* Excuse me?"

"Well, you could start with your clothes. You're wearing too much; you're more fabric than you are body. And it should be the opposite."

"*That's* your brilliant advice?" I rolled my eyes. "Anyone can wear less clothes, that does not a hot girl make." Without thinking about it, I reached for the bottle and refilled my glass halfway.

"I wasn't finished."

"Oh, well then, please, I'm on the edge of my seat." I scooted up to the actual edge of my seat and pantomimed dramatic intrigue.

"Do you actually want my advice? I don't want to be that dick who gives unsolicited opinions."

"Don't you think it's a bit too late for that?"

"You're right, I'm sorry. Forget I said anything."

"No, I want to know. I can take it. I'm a *tough* girl, remember?"

"All right, then. If you got a Brazilian blowout, your hair wouldn't be so, you know, crazy or whatever. Guys dig the silky hair thing." He looked at me cautiously until I nodded for him to go on. "And then, you know, just wear some makeup. Some lip color and smoky eyes make a big difference. But not too much, it's gross when girls wear too much makeup, doesn't look natural. Oh!" He snapped two fingers and pointed at me. "And a push-up bra. You have great tits, but no one is ever gonna know that unless you get some good cleavage going on."

Who the hell is this guy? I thought. *And who does he think he is giving beauty advice when he himself is no higher than a four and looks like he hasn't showered in days?* Little did he know I cared about a whole lot of things, but what men thought of me was not on the list.

"Such wisdom." I shook my head slowly, playing goofily at being in awe. "And from someone so young."

I impressed myself, thinking quickly, moving breezily over my words. I was flowing through the moments the way the scotch was flowing through my blood effortlessly.

"Well, believe me, you got what it takes. But it's not just that you're cute."

"Oh no?"

"It's just who you are. As far as girls go, you're super real."

"Unlike all the other girls who're . . . holograms?"

"You know what I mean."

"Actually, I don't. But I'd like to. What's real about me? In your opinion."

"Fuck, Justine, I don't know." He finished his cigarette and put it out. "Girls like to put on a show, say all the right things at the right time with the right tone of voice, it gets exhausting just watching them. It's like . . ."

He lit another cigarette. "It's like they've created masks of who they think they're supposed to be, and they've worn the masks so long that they've become a part of their actual faces, and maybe they don't even know the difference anymore between their faces and the masks. Makes for a great Instagram following, though. And they live for that shit."

"*Really?* This coming from the guy who just told me to doll myself up?"

"That's different," he explained. "It's good to look sexy, we like that, but then that perfect, composed hotness sinks into their insides and paralyzes their personalities. You know, sort of how Botox can freeze your face muscles so that you can't really smile."

"So, the dream girl is put together on the outside but raw and earnest on the inside."

"Pretty much."

"That's a tall order, Zan." I held back my profound irritation and did my best to keep it sounding like convivial banter. "How would you feel if we held you to such high standards? Think you'd pass the test?"

He glanced down at his bare torso, then laughed.

"I never said I had the full package," he defended himself. "But I don't pretend to be something I'm not the way all these girls do. Everything with them is *perfect*—never *bad* or *disappointing* or even plain old *good*. It all has to be *perfect*. Perfect or *special*. They want you to think they fly above the pitfalls of human nature, so they compose and curate themselves to hide that they're lonely just like the rest of us. Sometimes I wonder if there's anything underneath that mask at all." He shivered at the thought. "Like what if I pulled it back and there was nothing there, just vapor?"

"Maybe that's what you want."

"Meaning . . . ?"

"I mean, maybe you prefer the idea that there's nothing under the mask, because if her tailored facade is all she has, then she's not intimidating, she's not a threat."

"I'm not *threatened* by these girls," he insisted. "I want to get to know them, like, know who they *really* are, but they won't let their guards down. Ever. They won't let anyone in."

"So they stay a mystery to you." I began to understand. "They seem too perfect to be 'real.'"

"Exactly."

"But not me. *I* don't seem too perfect to be real."

I decided *real girl* wasn't a compliment at all. It was just another way of labeling girls and putting them into controllable categories, pitting them against each other. It was just a sneakier way of saying, *women are somewhat inferior to men.* Because, of course, the subtext of *real girl* is that while all men are real, the average woman is not.

I suspected that *real girl*, at least for Zander, meant the same thing as *one of the guys*. In other words: a girl demystified, stripped of her feminine power, a butterfly without wings, much easier to catch, play with, and grow bored of.

"No." He let the right side of his mouth curl into a smile. "You're perfect in an entirely different way."

I couldn't think of what to say to this, so I said nothing. He leaned in over the table and took my hands, leaving the cigarette dangling from his bottom lip.

"Hey." I was desperate to change the subject and I knew just how to do it. "Can I ask you a question?"

"Anything."

"What's the deal with Ruby?"

"How do you mean?"

"I mean what's her deal . . . like, who is she and what does she . . . do? Who are all these guys? Do you all work for her, or—?"

"Well, well." Ruby walked in just then, Eva-Kate close behind. "Looks like you two are getting along."

Zander dropped my hands like they were hot coals. I saw his tattoo again; it was grainy and perforated, like it had been done by hand.

"Just making her feel at home, Ruby," he said apologetically.

"Of course you were, baby, and I'm sure you've done a truly stand-up job."

Zander liked hearing this; he smiled bashfully and looked down at his feet.

"We should go, Justine," Eva-Kate said. "Josie's starting to blow up my phone."

"Wouldn't want to upset the wife." Ruby winked deviously.

"You're terrible." Eva-Kate playfully slapped Ruby's arm.

"It was a dream to see you, as always." Ruby kissed Eva-Kate on each of her cheeks. "And so special to meet you, Justine."

Zander gave me a secretive *I told you so* glance.

"It was great meeting you too," I said, finding my footing. "And thank you."

"You know your way out, yes?" Ruby clasped her hands and held them in front of her heart. I found this funny; she said it as if her home was a complex network of wings and corridors, when actually the house entrance was visible from where we stood in the kitchen doorway. Eva-Kate said she did, and grabbed my hand, practically dragging me to the door. At the last minute I turned around and saw Zander look away from Ruby just long enough to wink at me, and then we were gone.

❋ ❋ ❋

"What was that about?" Eva-Kate asked, pulling back onto the freeway.

"Me?! I could ask you the same thing!" Princess Leia was chewing on her own paw and had hardly acknowledged our return.

"Are you drunk?" She pointed an amused finger at me.

"Buzzed," I corrected her. "Lagavulin 16." I loved the way it sounded, how the words fit in my mouth.

"Did he kiss you? He's not allowed, you know. Ruby would flip."

"I think he was about to."

"Did you want him to?"

"Gross, no. I don't want my first kiss to be with some random, greasy . . . manservant."

I wouldn't have said this sober, and I regretted it immediately.

"*First* kiss?"

"Well, yeah, I'm—"

"Oh my God, are you . . . you've never—"

"No, I haven't, okay? I'm sixteen, it's not a big deal."

"I just can't even imagine," she said. "I mean, I lost my virginity almost five years ago."

"When you were *twelve*?"

"No, God. Thirteen. Oh, but don't tell anyone that, a good chunk of the country thinks I'm saving myself for marriage." She rolled her eyes. "Gotta keep up the act for all those naive middle America hypocrites or whatever."

"Great, sure, yeah, you got it. Are we just not going to

talk about why you left me alone with some guy I've never met?"

"Zander? Oh, babycakes, I would never leave you alone with someone I didn't trust. Zander practically lives to keep Ruby and her friends safe. He wouldn't hurt a fly. Well, unless the fly provoked him, I suppose."

"Why did you need to be alone with Ruby?"

"Don't be mad at me, jeez. It's not some big deal! Ruby does psychic readings and the room needs to be clear of any extra energies, otherwise it won't work."

"Then why couldn't you just say so?"

"Uh, well, because I thought you'd think I was stupid for being into this stuff. And anyway, pessimism also gets in the way of a good reading."

"I wouldn't think it's stupid," I said grumpily. "I used to go to a psychic."

I didn't mention that this psychic was actually my first roommate at Bellflower. An illiterate girl named April who refused to take her meds and analyzed the lines in my palms at night. In exchange I read aloud to her about fruit bats from an issue of *Zoobooks* that she'd stolen from the common room. One time she told me that in a past life I was Abraham Lincoln. I told her that psychics are supposed to tell the future, not the past, and to that she replied, "Fine, then in the *future* you're going to be Abraham Lincoln."

"Well, I didn't know that, did I?" Eva-Kate said then. "And I didn't want to risk it."

"What did she tell you? Anything interesting?"

"Yes, as a matter of fact. She said you're the only person I should trust."

"Me?"

"Yeah."

"Me, Justine? I'm the only person you should trust?"

"Yes, Jesus! What's so crazy about that? Is she wrong?"

"No, not at all. She's one hundred percent right. I mean, I don't know about everyone else, but I do know I'm trustworthy. And that you can trust me."

"Good, because she also said I should invite you to move in with me. And I agree."

"Wait, what? Why would you even want that?"

"Why *wouldn't* I? I need people close to me who I can trust. Loyal people. And if Ruby says you're the only one, then I'm really going to need you. And besides, I have so much empty space in that house I don't know what to do with it all. I need new positive energies and memories to make it feel like home."

"What about your friends? Josie and Olivia . . . London, aren't they loyal?"

"Hardly," Eva-Kate sighed. "Olivia and London are human parasites, and Josie . . . well, sometimes I just don't know. And when it comes to loyalty, I don't like not knowing."

"Can I bring Princess Leia?" It was a dumb thing to

ask, I knew that immediately, but I was at a loss for any other words.

"Obviously. I love that weird little dog; she brought you to me, didn't she?"

"I guess so, in a way."

"So is this a yes or a no? You can have the guest bedroom and you can wear any clothes you find in that closet; it's all stuff I don't vibe with anymore. Sound good, fam?"

"Yes, definitely yes."

"Oh, and remember we have the party tomorrow."

"What party?"

"*Pool party?*" she reminded me. "*Taylor Swift?*"

"That's *tomorrow*?" I scanned the past week in my mind, trying to calculate today's date. I realized the days since school let out had blended together in an indecipherable blur.

"Sure is, doll face. I only RSVP'd because *you* wanted to go, and you're my plus-one so it would be pretty lame to bail on me."

"I'm not bailing! Are you kidding me? I would never."

Satisfied, Eva-Kate leaned back against the headrest and looked up at the moon roof, then pressed the button to make it slide open, uncovering tufts of cumulus clouds backed by ambrosial sunlight.

CHAPTER 12

SQUAD

Taylor Swift, Eva-Kate had said. *Are you a fan?*

This very simple question had baffled me for almost half my life.

I can't say that I'm a Taylor Swift fan, exactly, but I also can't say that I'm not. I'd be lying if I said I wasn't totally hooked on each and every one of her six albums, but it's not as if you'll find me at her stadium shows holding up a sign with I ♥ TAYLOR written in pink glitter, tears streaming down my face.

I find her lyrics to be naive, bordering on delusional, stubborn in their sentimentality, unapologetically confessional, all of it shameless. And she is, at least what she shows the public, a human representation of those lyrics. Both in business and her personal life she is unforgiving, bordering on petty, constantly walking the line between self-respect and abuse of power. And yet these things about her that make me cringe are also qualities I admire so much that they haunt me. When, in "All Too Well" (a lesser-known song from *Red*), she sings, "But you keep my old scarf from that very first week, cuz it reminds you of innocence and it smells like me," I think: *Wow, how overly confident, how nice it must feel to be so blindly trusting, to believe oneself to be unforgettable, whether true or not.* And when, in "Shake It Off," a hit from *1989*, she sings, "It's like I've got this music in my mind saying it's gonna be all right," I think: *Wow, where can I get some of that music?*

What I'm saying is, since I'm trying my best to tell this story as truthfully and as thoroughly as I can, I need to confess that during that summer (and, actually, the nine years leading up to it) I thought about Taylor Swift—her music, her look, her love life, the astronomic rise of her career—way more than makes logical sense. Does that make me psycho? Sure, I don't know, maybe.

✳ ✳ ✳

I was back at home after the drive up from San Onofre listening to *Fearless*, the 2008 follow-up to her first eponymous (and platinum) album released in 2006. I hadn't slept in thirty-three hours. I'd surpassed exhaustion and was soaring with the illusion of limitless energy. I knew I should sleep, but my mind was reeling, bouncing from thought to thought, visual to visual—Eva-Kate's periwinkle car, the diamond *J* on her Juicy Couture zipper, Dennis talking to her in the darkened hallway, Ruby's fingernails, her crystals, the strange DIY tattoo on Zander's wrist, the translucent green whiskey bottles lined up in a row, Eva-Kate dropping me off behind my parents' house and telling me to pack a bag—so I'd stayed awake all night, lying in the dark looking up at a ceiling of glow-in-the-dark stars, nervous that if I fell asleep I'd wake up to find it had all been a dream.

I felt a million years away from that little girl outside of Rachel Ames's trailer, like I'd finally vanquished her. I wanted to turn the volume all the way up, to get naked and dance to the contagious country pop, but now that I knew Eva-Kate could see into my house from her roof, I couldn't shake the feeling I was being watched. Sure, I'd closed all the curtains and blinds, but after knowing her for almost two days I knew that if anyone were capable of having X-ray vision, it would be Eva-Kate Kelly.

So I kept the music low and my clothes on, humming along to the songs as I tossed my belongings into a JanSport backpack, ignoring the text messages from Riley that kept popping up on my phone.

We're going to Swingers for milkshakes. Meet us there.

Are you coming?

Are you being weird on purpose or do you not realize you're being weird?

Abbie says you're a bitch.

Text us back, bitch. So we know you're alive etc.

I turned the sound off and stumbled to my closet, filling my backpack with underwear and T-shirts and my collection of Bonne Bell lip gloss and the blossom-scented foaming face wash that was the only one that wouldn't make me break out, a toothbrush, and my antianxiety meds I could never go more than two days without.

From the living room I packed a ziplock bag of food for Princess Leia and a full carton of Marlboro Reds I found in the cabinet above her food, gathering dust. I absentmindedly attributed them to being a relic of my father's first midlife crisis in 2010 and tossed them into the backpack, hoping that arriving at Eva-Kate's with my own cigarettes would help her to see me as an equal, or at least not as the cherub I imagined she imagined me to be. Zipping up the backpack, a sharp, silvery glimmer caught the corner of my eye. It was the overhead light ricocheting off the crystal doors of my dad's liquor cabinet. Inspired, I emptied a water bottle and surveyed my options. My eyes bounced from Grey Goose to Stolichnaya to Smirnoff to Jim Beam to Johnnie Walker to Jack Daniel's. On the whiskey bottles I looked for the words SINGLE MALT but couldn't find them, so I went with Johnnie Walker Red. The bottle slid easily into my backpack like a missing piece.

✳ ✳ ✳

"Welcome home, babycakes," Eva-Kate said when I arrived the next morning around ten. She was wearing a sheer cotton T-shirt and black interlock running shorts, her pink hair in disarray and yesterday's makeup smudged around her eyes.

She'd told me to come by with my stuff whenever, and I figured going over immediately would seem desperate. So I waited out the night, watching season three of *Jennie and Jenny*, feeling myself drift in and out of sleep.

She took my backpack and handed it to a man—at least six feet tall and significantly built—wearing a blue button-down shirt rolled up around his bulging forearms. "This is Homer, head of security, he keeps the crazies out. Homer, this is Justine; will you take this backpack up to her room, please?"

"Nice to meet you, Justine," he said. "And of course, Miss Kelly, right away."

"It's *Eva-Kate*, Homer!" she corrected him, teetering on the edge of flirtation. "*Please*, we're practically family."

"Whatever you say, Eva-Kate." He smiled modestly and headed upstairs.

"I don't like treating my staff like servants," she said to me once he was gone. "Really creeps me out. Sure, they work for me, but I would *so much* prefer it if they didn't." She walked me into the kitchen, where she offered me a seat on a teetering bar stool and turned on an espresso maker.

"You wish you didn't have people working for you?"

"It's just not normal." She wrinkled her nose and hopped onto the stool beside mine. "I'm seventeen and I have a *staff*. And I pay them a salary just to take care of me. Like advanced-level babysitters. My manager says I can't fire them, that I need them, so I'll sometimes say, *Hey, buddy, I can fire you too, you know!* But he reminds me that then a whole bunch of people would be out of jobs and I just feel too guilty to do that to them after all they've done for me. So I keep them on and I guess everyone's happy. Except me, because I hate being treated like a porcelain doll all the damn time. I'm capable, you know? See, look, I can make espresso all by myself and everything!" She brought me a china teacup filled halfway with steaming, frothy espresso. Had I asked for espresso? Had she offered it to me? I didn't think so.

"Thank you," I said, taking it from her. "But I guess it's still smart to have security, right? To keep the crazies out, like you said. And there must be a lot of them."

"I *guess*." She rolled her eyes, making herself a double shot. "But I have cameras all over the property and they're being monitored constantly by the Elite Security central offices in Hollywood. They could press a button and have police here faster than you could say Jiminy Cricket. Who is Jiminy Cricket anyway?"

"He was the cricket from *Pinocchio*," I said, imagining what it would be like to have a security team, to *need* a security team. "He represented Pinocchio's conscience."

"Oh, well," she said, downing the piping-hot espresso in one gulp, "enough about that, we don't have much time. Little Miss Swifty's party starts at four and I'd say we should get there around five thirty."

"That . . . sorry, but doesn't that actually give us, like . . . *many* hours to get ready?"

"Yep." She slid off the bar stool so that her shorts rose up, revealing the soft flesh at the very top of her thigh, so snowy white, even compared to the rest of her body. "And we'll need every second."

CHAPTER 13

IMITATIONS AND KNOCKOFFS

*H*eads turned to Eva-Kate as we walked into the Roosevelt Hotel lobby off Hollywood Boulevard. She wore a gold lamé halter minidress and six-inch heels with star-spangled straps, gold glitter eye makeup, and a gold tiara fastened with gold silk roses.

I caught my reflection in a mirror behind the reception desk and didn't recognize myself. Eva-Kate dressed me from head to toe in items from her closet: an American-red Herve Leger bandage dress, art deco rings on every finger, black leather Chloé wedges with rose-gold rivets along the soles. She'd even called hair and makeup to give me smoky-red eyes and a keratin-enriched blowout.

I'd never walked in heels before, and so far it wasn't going too well; I wobbled behind Eva-Kate, who had to grab my hand several times to keep me from toppling over. London and Olivia tried to stifle their laughter; Josie kept wincing, as if it were painful just to watch me. When Eva-Kate had said I'd be her plus-one, I naively assumed it would be just the two of us. I hadn't considered that the rest of the gang had received their own invites. I wished I could make them disappear. They were tiresome accessories, useless as eight of my ten art deco rings.

Outside on the pool deck, the party was in full swing. Lean bodies in summer dresses and string bikinis, swim trunks and Speedos, moved around each other and with each other, seamlessly and gracefully like a choreographed dance. This was nothing like any party I'd been to, or even the ones I'd seen in movies. People here were practiced in their movements, they held their chins up high, they had reputations to maintain, they held their drinks like prized novelty items, not like devices of mental obliteration. Even with the sun bright and high, flamingo-pink lights shone up from the bases of palm trees, matching the cabana curtains on the opposite end of the pool.

"Closer" by the Chainsmokers featuring Halsey blasted from speakers suspended on all four corners of the deck. I counted fourteen flower crowns in just the first three minutes. Ordinarily this would be the type of situation to send me into a panic—the claustrophobia, the intrusive noise, the feeling of terminal inferiority—but Eva-Kate held on to my hand and Taylor Swift was somewhere nearby, so for once in my life I felt lifted above it all.

"Isn't this song extremely two summers ago?" Eva-Kate asked me very seriously, as if I were the official record keeper of one-hit wonders. "I wish if they'd go retro they'd go all the way retro. Would it kill them to put on some Foo Fighters? 'Everlong' is a forgotten classic, totally timeless. *This* just feels stale."

"Eva-Kate!" Spencer Sawyer jumped at us before I had a moment to answer, neon-green baseball cap on backward. He held up his camera and on instinct, Eva-Kate struck a pose. FLASH! It was broad daylight, there was absolutely no need for flash, but that's how his photos got their ultra-bright hyperreal vibes.

"Get one with me and Justine," she said, looping her arm around my waist, hardly acknowledging him at all.

"You got it," he said, lifting the camera again. As he did so, Eva-Kate turned and pressed her lips against my cheek. I felt the kiss leave an oily mark and chose to wear it as a badge of honor.

"Where's my insufferable girlfriend?" he asked, letting the camera dangle around his neck.

"I dunno, she was just right here. Probably went to the bathroom with Olivia. I'd walk on eggshells if I were you, she's in quite the mood. Both of them are, actually."

"What else is new?" he asked, and the two shared an amused, I'm-so-over-it kind of glance.

"Got us a table over there." Josie came up behind us and pointed to an umbrella-shaded table next to the DJ booth.

"Let's do it, then." Eva-Kate wasted no time. "The sooner we're seen, the sooner we can leave. And if we *make* a scene, we can leave even sooner."

I didn't want to leave, and I didn't want to make a scene at this party of all places, but I had no intention of doing anything that would go against Eva-Kate's flow.

London and Olivia joined us with freshly applied makeup. They now wore matching green glitter eye shadow and so much clear lip gloss you could almost see the pool reflected on their pouty mouths. And Eva-Kate had been right, Olivia could not pull off a cloche hat.

"They do this matching makeup thing," Spencer said to no one in particular, snapping a photo as the two girls sat down. "It's like so people know they came here with someone, that they're not alone."

"What?" London laughed. "That's not true."

"Yeah," said Spencer, "it is. This psychologist on *Dr. Phil* said girls will do this to demonstrate they're part of a tribe. So that other people know not to fuck with them. It's an insecurity thing, goes back to cave people times. Can't argue with it."

"Ah yes, well, if Dr. Phil said it." London rolled her eyes.

"Nothing like being *mansplained* to by a guy who sits on the couch all day watching *Dr. Phil*," Olivia added.

"Hey, it's the sitting on the couch all day that allows me to go all night long."

"Charming." Eva-Kate frowned.

A waitress in candy-apple-red booty shorts came by, balancing a tray of brightly colored drinks.

"Mojitos," she said, setting the tray down carefully in the center of our table and gesturing showgirl style to the various colors. "These ones are blueberry, these ones are cucumber, these ones are . . . *mango*, and these ones are raspberry, 'K? I'm Desirée, let me know if y'all need anything else."

"Thaaaanks, Desirée," Josie singsonged while the rest of us reached for a mojito. Mine was blueberry. I was too queasy to drink from it, so I chewed lightly on the straw instead. Blueberries and shreds of mint floated through rum and syrup.

"Justine, you have some lipstick on your cheek," London said, reaching over to wipe it off. Without meaning to, I jerked away.

"Don't you want me to get it for you?"

"It's okay, I'll—"

"I like it," Eva-Kate interrupted. "It gives her an air of mystery and nonchalance. Makes you wonder who kissed her and why she doesn't care to wipe it off."

"No it doesn't," said Olivia. "*You* kissed her. It's very obvious that you kissed her."

"Sure, maybe—"

"It's the exact shade you're wearing," London noted.

"Nice work, *detective*." Eva-Kate gave her minions that familiar, crucifying bored-to-tears glance over her sunglasses as she stirred her mango mojito.

"Justine, look over here," Spencer said. "I need a solo shot of you for the site. Sort of like a 'meet Justine' type intro for the fans."

I turned to him and smiled mechanically like this was for a yearbook photo. FLASH! FLASH! FLASH! He snapped three in a row, leaving me blinded.

"Babycakes, don't smile for him," Eva-Kate advised. "You should always look like a camera in your face is a nuisance, like you have somewhere to be and this is wasting your time."

"Don't listen to her, Justine." Spencer kept snapping and I made sure to pout, even scowl. "She's bitter and jaded. Everyone loves a big smile."

"First of all, it's not about what everyone loves. If you give everyone what they love, they own you. Fuck *everyone*. Second of all, okay, stop, you're gonna hurt her eyes." Eva-Kate put her hands out in front of his lens until eventually he gave up. I blinked and blinked, trying to make the spots of silvery light go away. Suddenly it felt very bright out. I closed my eyes to try to reset.

"Here, take my glasses." Eva-Kate lifted the Tom Ford

sunglasses off her face and put them on mine. Then everything was softened with a nice, muted green tint.

"Thanks, that's much better."

"Goddamn, those look good on you." She leaned back to admire me and seemed proud of herself. "You should def keep them."

"*Keep them?* No, these are thousand-dollar glasses, at *least.* I couldn't."

"Actually"—she leaned in closer so that only I could hear—"they're fake."

"What do you mean?"

"They're knockoffs. I bought them online for like fifteen dollars."

"Really? But they look so . . . legit."

"I *know,*" she practically gushed. "That's what makes it so beautiful."

"I don't . . . understand," I confessed.

"Okay, you're gonna think I'm a freak," she warned me, "but I absolutely *adore* knockoffs. Of all kinds. Purses, glasses, watches, jewelry, you name it. They've always been so much more exciting to me than their 'authentic' counterparts."

"I think I get that. Is it because they're kind of like . . . a lie? And if they're good imitations, then they're a lie you can get away with?"

"I never thought of it that way, but sure, yeah, that's part of the appeal. But it's more than that. Nine out of ten times the knockoffs actually last longer than the originals. Designers can effortlessly put out whatever product they want, and everyone will buy it just for the label, it's an easy sell. Meanwhile, the swindlers have to work twice as hard to create a believable imitation, so the knockoffs end up with double the effort put into them, and are often so much more durable because of it. Almost nobody knows this, because anyone who can afford the original isn't gonna bother slumming it with knockoffs, and anyone who can only afford knockoffs will never be able to splurge on an original."

"That's true . . . ," I said, and then backed off. I wanted to hear more. I loved her weird, confident plans and opinions; they were weird and confident plans that nobody else had.

"And the way I see it, the knockoffs are so good at imitating the originals that they're actually more impressive as an art form, the process by which they're created is so much more intricate and nuanced. I guess what I'm trying to say is that sometimes imitation is an art, while simply designing a purse for people to carry around just isn't. And if the imitation version is an artistic feat and it functions better than the original, then tell me, which one is real and which is fake?"

"Wow." I hadn't realized her capacity for philosophical thought, and this was one I knew would haunt me for some time. "You're right. Who's to say what's real and what's fake, anyway? Who gets to define those words?"

"Exactly." She pinched my cheek. "Of course you

understand. You're my fucking gemstone, that's what you are."

Blood and heat rushed to my cheeks in a blush so forceful it almost hurt.

Then, across the pool, emerging from a cabana, I caught a glimpse of brilliantly blond hair and cardinal-red lips, a bikini—yellow and white stripes—on a buoyant, gazelle-like body. It was Taylor. Swift. It was Taylor Swift in the flesh.

"*There* she is," said Eva-Kate, making a visor with her hand as she looked across the pool. "Come on, I'll introduce you."

"No." Involuntarily, I gripped on to the white plastic arms of my chair. "I can't."

"You *can't*?"

"I mean"—I lowered my voice to a whisper—"it's *Taylor Swift*."

"So? She's just a person, Justine, she's not God."

"I know, but—"

"Let's go, we have to desensitize you, celebrity worship doesn't look good on *anyone*, trust me." She grabbed on to my wrist and pulled me up with her. "Plus, I can't have a girl in *my* squad so mesmerized by Taylor fucking Swift."

My squad. I was *in* Eva-Kate Kelly's squad. Suddenly I knew she was right: There was no reason to have Taylor on a pedestal. *She's just a person.*

"You're right, you're right." I laughed. "Let's do it."

But as we made our way around the perimeter of the pool, a new party guest arrived, and from the looks of it, he brought a date. It was Rob Donovan and . . . Eva-Kate? I stopped dead in my tracks: The girl with Rob looked almost identical to the girl whose hand was now holding my wrist. She seemed to weigh a bit more than Eva-Kate, and her hair was somewhat darker, and she wore wire-framed glasses, but her face . . . She had the exact same face . . .

"Why'd you stop walking?" Eva-Kate asked. Then she saw what I saw. "Oh, fuck me sideways," she said under her breath. "I don't believe it."

"Who is that?"

"My ex, Rob Donovan."

"I know who Rob Donovan is. I mean who is he with?"

"Liza," she sighed. "My sister."

CHAPTER 14

GETTING THE HELL OUT OF HERE IS PRICELESS

"*Y*ou have a sister?" I stared. "An *identical twin sister?*"

Eva-Kate ushered me to an open table and manipulated the adjoined umbrella so that we were hidden.

"*Obviously,*" she said, like having to explain this was the biggest inconvenience of her life.

I sat back and tried to figure out how I hadn't known this. A memory flickered into formation: Mary-Kate and Ashley Olsen played one role on *Full House*. They were credited as Mary-Kate Ashley Olsen as if it were one long name, and it was years before people realized Michelle Tanner was played by two different girls.

"Oh my God," I said. "Of course you have a twin. Child labor laws . . ."

"State that children ages three to seven can only work for six hours a day, four days a week. Maximum. *Jennie and Jenny*, like most shows, would need me to work all five days. So they had to cast twins. It's not uncommon."

"I don't know why I never thought about that. I mean, I *knew* that shows do it."

"But one year into the show we turned eight and the rules weren't as strict. Eight-year-olds can work *five* days a week for up to *eight* hours, and she desperately wanted out, so then it was just me. Of the nine years *Jennie and Jenny* was on the air, Liza only acted in one season."

"Liza," I repeated, "right. That's the name you . . . wait, but I thought you said it was Liza McKelvoy?" I remembered her in the Little Beach House hallway, coercing information out of that poor waiter.

"Yep." She closed and opened her eyes. "That's her."

"But your last name is—"

"Also McKelvoy," she confirmed. "'Kelly' is just a cuter version. My agent came up with it after Liza dropped out. I liked it right away; McKelvoy never really felt like me."

"Wow." It was a lot to process. "So you have a twin sister who isn't an actress."

"She hates acting. Everything about it. I've honestly been kind of impressed with how well she's managed to stay out of the spotlight. She's a hostess. Most people don't even know she exists."

"Right. She used to work at the Little Beach House but now she works at Chateau Marmont. So that means Rob's new song is about . . ."

"That's right," Eva-Kate said sadly. "I'd be lying if I said I didn't hate her."

"I'm sorry, that's awful."

"Not really," she assured me. "She hates me too. It's always been like this."

I didn't see how this made things any less awful, but I nodded compassionately. I wanted to put my hand on hers and find a way to let her know that it was going to be okay, that one day she'd forget about Rob and looking back on all this would make her laugh. She looked into my eyes then and gave me a slow, deeply thankful smile, then quickly kissed me on the cheek.

"Thank you so much for listening to me rant," she said. "Now it's time to face the music."

"What do you—"

"Look, they're already talking to my friends. *My* friends. Oh, come on, *Olivia.*" She spied on their table from behind our umbrella. "Don't engage."

I looked over and saw Olivia offering Rob a seat. He declined, slipping his arm around Liza's waist. She was wearing black jeans and a faded blue T-shirt, sandals that looked like they could be from Target.

"How's my makeup?" Eva-Kate looked into me like a mirror. Her makeup was impeccable, not a line out of place; every color adhered to her face as if she were born with it.

"It's perfect. What are we doing?"

She stood up and rolled her neck a few times in each direction.

"We're going over there, acting like everything is totally copacetic, okay? We're acting like we couldn't possibly care less. When I introduce you, you'll act like you've never heard of either of them . . . act like you're having too much fun with me to even notice them, got it?"

"Yep. Got it," I said, though I was troubled by how many times she'd used the word *act*. I had zero acting skills, and knew somehow I'd mess this up.

"What's that?" she asked.

"What's what?"

"That vibrating. Is that your phone?"

I heard it then, the aggravated buzzing coming from my purse.

"Oh." I peered at the screen without taking it out. "It's . . . my dad. He never calls me."

"Answer it."

"But I thought no phones?"

"Take it out to the parking lot, it's fine. Just meet me back at the table when you're done. And remember, act disinterested."

"Right." I nodded. "Disinterested."

She flipped her hair off her shoulders and walked

away, headed for the table where Rob and Liza were hovering uncomfortably. She walked so calmly, hips swaying slightly from side to side, her fingers wiggling a vague hello as she approached them. Luckily for her, unlike me, she was a very convincing actress.

"Hold on, Dad, give me five minutes." I answered the phone, then slipped it back into my bag and backtracked through the lobby, out into the parking lot where the valet boys were organizing the black and white luxury cars like a game of Tetris. "Okay, hey, what's up?"

"What's *up*? I haven't heard from you in two weeks, *that's* what's up."

"I haven't heard from you either," I deflected. "I was waiting for you to call me. Mom said you would."

"Oh, *Mom said*," he repeated. "Well, then."

"Yeah." I didn't have anything else to say—what was I supposed to say? He'd decided to divorce my mom without telling me; he'd moved all his stuff out without saying goodbye.

"Have you been taking care of yourself?"

"Yes," I shot back. "Have you?"

He sighed, crackly through the speaker. I could hear the sound of liquid being poured and ice rattling against glass. Distant and muffled, but unmistakable.

"Look, I'm a little worried about you, bumblebee."

"Me? Why?" He hadn't said something like this in years. My heart skipped a paranoid beat.

"I ran into Christopher at Erewhon and he said he's seen you going over to the house across the way."

"Christopher our *neighbor*? What were you even doing at the Venice Erewhon?" I surprised myself by being mildly hurt that he'd been in Venice and not bothered to come see me. "And what, is Christopher spying on me now?"

"He's not spying on you, don't be dramatic, little bird. He lives right there and he happened to see you go over there two or three times."

"And? So?"

"Supposedly some famous actress girl lives there now? Are you spending time with her? I hope you're being careful."

"Careful? What if I *am* spending time with her?"

"You're just a kid, JuJu, I don't want you living too fast. Famous kids, girls like Ava Kelly, they're bright stars but they burn out fast. It never turns out well for them."

"It's *Eva-Kate Kelly*," I corrected him. "And I'm not her. She's just a friend."

"I just wouldn't want to see you get pulled into that mess."

"What mess? There is no mess."

"Drugs, parties, booze. We've always trusted you to make the right decisions. Can we still trust that?"

"Absolutely. Yep. No parties, no drugs, no booze. Got it."

"You could move in with me for a bit until your mother gets—"

"No, no, no, that's really not necessary. Promise. Nothing's changed, I'm still the same person. You should be happy for me, you wouldn't actually want me to spend all my time with Aunt Jillian, would you?"

"Well . . . no. But you're sure you're being safe?"

"Yes."

"And you're eating vegetables?"

"Yes."

"And you're exercising?"

"Uh . . . sure. Yes."

"Okay, just make sure to take your vitamins."

"I will. Dad, I gotta go, we'll talk soon, okay?"

"Okay, okay. And remember to brush your teeth."

"My teeth? Dad, I'm not five."

"Sure, but—"

"'K, Dad, gotta go. Love you."

I hung up and took a deep breath.

"He's right, you know." I spun around and saw Rob Donovan leaning against the metal fence separating us from the pool. How long had he been standing behind me? How much had he heard? What had I even said?

"Sorry?" I asked, playing dumb, but also feeling dumb. He lit an American Spirit.

"You're too sweet to get caught up in Eva-Kate's whirlwind world of mayhem."

Whirlwind world of mayhem? Wow, he really *did* fancy himself a poet.

"You don't know that." I folded my arms.

"Then you're *not* a total sweetheart? Sure, I guess you can't judge a book by its cover."

"Um, what exactly about all of this screams 'total sweetheart'?" I gestured at my outfit, the bandage dress and clunky wood-block wedges.

"What you're *wearing*?" He laughed. "Oh, I can see through all that. You're just a sweetheart in Eva-Kate's clothes."

"Whatever."

"Am I wrong?"

"I—I don't know."

"You don't have to," he said. "It's okay. Want a cigarette?"

"No, thanks, I told Eva-Kate I'd be back."

"What a good soldier."

"Sorry?"

"Eva-Kate is the general. You're one of her soldiers. A new recruit. You do what she says." He took a long drag. "And you're doing a great job."

"I'm not a soldier," I protested, though the word *squad* began to reverberate in my mind. "I'm her friend."

"Wanna know a secret?"

"Uh, not really."

"It's about Eva-Kate."

"Fine. What?"

"You'll actually get more of her attention if you stay here and have a cigarette with me."

"Her *attention*? I met her two days ago and she's already invited me to move in, so I think I've done a pretty okay job of getting her attention. But thanks."

"So you think once you're in, that's it? Are you actually *that* blinded by the light?"

"What do you mean?" He was trying to make me nervous but I didn't know why. It was starting to work.

"She has the attention span of a frog. Just because she's into you today doesn't mean she will be tomorrow. Her *besties* are just flavors of the week."

"That's not true. Josie and Ruby have been her closest friends forever."

"Maybe. Or maybe that's just what she says."

"Oh, give me a break," I said, trying not to latch onto the thought.

"You want her to like you, right? You think being a loyal friend will make her like you, and you think being a loyal friend means staying away from me, right?"

"You're her ex, aren't you?"

"But here's the irony: The more time you spend talking to me, the more attention you get from me, the closer she'll want you to her. She keeps her friends close, but she likes to keep her enemies even closer. You know what I mean?"

"Yeah, so?"

"So, the real way to secure your spot in her inner circle is to make her feel jealous . . . or threatened. Which you can do easily by staying out here to have a cigarette with me."

"I don't want to make Eva-Kate jealous," I said. "That's the last thing I'd want to do. Why would I want to be her enemy?"

"Like I just said: to secure your spot. To be in for good. Do you have a better plan?"

"A *plan*? No, I don't have a *plan*. Eva-Kate's my friend, I'm not trying to play games with her. Maybe you are, but I'm not."

"Ohhhh." The confusion on his face melted away and he smiled like he'd cracked some kind of code. "You actually care about her."

"Excuse me?"

"You actually want to be her friend. I'm not used to this. She gets so many star fucker girl groupie type people hanging on to her all the time, and she lives off that attention so she's more than happy to let a few of them tag along here and there, even though she knows they're just using her. Or at least I *think* she knows. So yeah, I thought that's what this was, you hanging out with Eva-Kate to advance your own career."

"I don't *have* a career." I laughed sourly. "I'm sixteen! And I'm not using her for anything. I genuinely like her."

I had to walk toward him so that I could get back to the lobby door, but he put his arm out to stop me. When he did so, I saw a small zigzag design imprinted on his forearm, the same one that Zander had on his wrist: VVVL

"You don't get it," he said, flicking his cigarette to the cement. "She's not who you think she is."

"Then who is she?" I quipped. *"Michael Corleone?"* His arm brushed against my torso and we locked eyes. For a moment all I could think about was how jealous Riley and the others would be if they could see.

"She's a puppet," he warned me. *"And* the puppeteer. The world would be a better place without her."

"That's . . . ," I muttered quietly. "That's not true."

"It is true. And I'll tell you one more thing that's true." He stroked the back of his hand against my cheek.

"And what's that?" I gulped, suddenly unable to move a muscle.

"I'd really like to kiss you now."

"What?" I jerked my head away, then stumbled backward. "What? Why? You're dating Liza and you just—are you insane?"

"I don't know . . ." He smiled. "Can you define *sanity?"*

"You're insane."

"Why? Because I want to kiss you? Is your self-esteem really that low?"

"You don't even know me, and . . ." *And you could kiss*

any girl, I wanted to say, *so why me?* I tried to quiet the voice that told me this made me special, the voice that was enjoying every second of it.

"You're refreshing, I know that much about you. You've lived a grounded life before meeting Eva-Kate, I can see that, and I like it. It's like a cool breeze."

"That's bullshit," I countered. "There's no way my boring, average life makes me appealing to you."

"Boring and average is underrated, Justine. You don't know what you have till it's gone."

"How do you know my name? I didn't tell you my name."

"You're Eva-Kate's newest golden girl, Justine. Word travels fast."

"So then, that's what you like about Liza? She's separate from your world of fame? She's uncorrupted by fame?"

"That's part of it."

"You like fame virgins? You think somehow we're better people? *Sweeter?*"

"*Fame virgins*"—his mouth curled in amusement—"*are* better people. You know that when you've been around fame long enough."

"If Liza's such a great person, then why would she date her sister's boyfriend anyway?"

"Because it wouldn't make any difference to Eva-Kate! Eva-Kate hated Liza long before I came around, and nothing Liza ever did could change that. Finally, she gave up, she got tired of being mistreated, and she agreed to give me a chance."

"I have to go," I said, feeling disoriented. "Thanks for the . . . words of wisdom. I guess." I walked quickly through the lobby, eagerly wanting to get back to Eva-Kate, to get reoriented. I didn't like Rob, and I didn't trust him. I regretted taking the time to let him get in my head.

Eva-Kate intercepted me at the indoor water fountain.

"We're leaving," she said, moving full speed ahead. "I'll call an Uber."

"Wait, wait." I held her back. "Rob's out there smoking."

"Wish I still smoked," she said, looking around for another way out. "I'll ask about a back exit."

"Don't you want to stay for the fireworks?" I asked, trying to be just the right amount of mildly funny.

"I can put on my own firework show for ten thousand dollars," she said. "Getting the hell out of this nightmare is priceless."

CHAPTER 15

WE WERE THE KNIFE

L iving at Eva-Kate's house began to feel like home. My room was down the hall from hers and overlooked the canal with its freshly painted paddle boats and canoes bobbing in the breeze, its honeysuckle vines and jacaranda trees in full bloom, fallen purple petals floating in the green water below.

With nothing to do and nowhere to be, I spent the days sleeping on and off, just like a cat, just like I'd always wanted, curling up wherever the strongest sunbeam landed. I took long bubble baths in the deepest tub I'd ever seen, curtains drawn and candles lit, sipping from a glass of whiskey, taste-testing the bottles in Eva-Kate's prodigious collection one by one. I quickly found that the smokier-tasting the scotch, the more I adored it, and the older the bottle, the more I felt I was strolling through a decadent heaven of my own design.

Photos of us together circled the internet, and my Instagram following shot up to twenty thousand overnight. *Star* printed the picture of us leaving the Roosevelt, me in a bandage dress and Tom Ford knockoffs scowling at them as Eva-Kate waved, and beneath it the caption read, "Is EKK's new BFF a dark influence?" *People* magazine printed a blurry picture of Eva-Kate leaving Rite Aid with me at her side and the caption "EKK's late night ice cream run with mystery friend." Kids from school who'd never spoken to me came out of the woodwork. When I wasn't "babycakes," Eva-Kate started calling me Mystery Friend, and sometimes Dark Influence. We laughed at the absurdity: *me*? A dark influence on *her*?

"It's funny, 'cause you're such a babycake," she'd say. "Such a sweetheart."

Just like Rob had said.

So they thought I was a sweetheart. I wondered what they'd say if they knew the truth.

In the evenings, around five or six, Eva-Kate would burst through my door with a whirlwind of plans. She'd jabber eagerly, stumbling over her words, outlining the places we'd go and people we'd see that night. But we would never be more than thirty minutes out in the world before the plan started taking sharp turns and sudden twists. Tearing up Sunset in her periwinkle Audi, Eva-Kate would get a call or a text or a rush of inspiration and we'd be headed in the opposite direction faster than I had time to figure out what was happening. Whatever her original plan was, it would be a distant memory by the end of the night; the blueprint never even resembled the memories we built. If the plan was to get drinks at Tower Bar, then hit up a party at Justin Bieber's house and wind up at the *Nylon* magazine pool party on the rooftop of the Standard hotel, we would actually drive halfway to Tower Bar but change directions and go to Musso & Frank for dirty martinis and meatball subs, then meet Josie and Olivia and London at Soho House West Hollywood and end up skinny-dipping in Harrison Ford's daughter's indoor pool. Or if the plan was to get acrylic nail extensions adorned with two-hundred-dollar nail art, then go dancing at Playhouse, we'd end up getting drunk at home, then Ubering to Dave & Buster's for grilled cheese and arcade games. If the plan was up, we went down. If the plan was down, we went up. And if the plan was a newly ripened peach, we were the knife, slicing it up into tiny pieces and feeding it to the birds.

I never could keep up. By 10:00 P.M. my eyelids would start to droop and I'd battle the desire for a place to rest my head. Every time new characters were introduced to the play of our night, I'd tense up, become so acutely aware of each one of my words and movements that I couldn't make myself speak. My self-consciousness was almost crippling, but the heightened stimulation of potential and possibility made it worth all the discomfort. No matter how socially anxious I'd been, no matter how many times I told myself I'd never put myself through it again, halfway through the next day I'd be thirsty for the adrenaline, counting the hours until I'd be thrust back into the lawless realm that existed outside myself.

Luckily for me, Eva-Kate's extended entourage mistook my stiffness and my silence to mean that I was aloof and unimpressed. And so they asked for me again and again, vying to win my warmth and approval. Little did they know I saw them as demigods and goddesses, that I perceived each and every one of them to have had a golden nugget of je ne sais quoi embedded in their chest plate at birth, a blessing for the chosen ones that I would never, ever have.

But soon enough I started to learn which substances would help me forget all my imagined shortcomings. Soon after that, I learned that pretty much any substance would do the trick. When Eva-Kate saw my energy fading, she'd feed me tiny lines of coke out of the palm of her hand, like she was a mama deer and I was her fawn. When we'd walk into a new scene, dozens of new eyes on us, and Eva-Kate could see me start to freeze, she'd unscrew her silver Tiffany's flask and hand it to me. Her initials were engraved into the fine, polished silver. She kept it stocked with Lagavulin 16, just for me.

With Eva-Kate and her arsenal of potions at my side, I learned to relax. I let go of dread and learned to go with the flow. I closed my eyes and put my hands in the air as she sped recklessly along Mulholland with the moon roof open and the windows down. I posed giddily for anyone who wanted a picture, developing my own signature pose: demure and submissive, eyes low, hand on one hip and a coy smile on my whiskey-stung lips. I flirted clumsily with movie directors and record producers dangling shiny opportunities on a hook. I knew their offers were empty, nothing but tried and true attempts to take me home. But I didn't care; it wasn't them or their lies that I wanted, it was the thrill of conversing with people who spent money like it was blood, guaranteed to regenerate over and over ad infinitum. It was the high of being included where I'd always secretly suspected I belonged: on a modern-day, nonfiction Mount Olympus, in a realm of passwords and access codes, of red rope and red carpet, of exclusivity and people so accustomed to exclusivity they hardly recognized it anymore.

My favorite nights were the nights we'd stumble home at dawn and Eva-Kate would take my hands, whining, "I don't want to be alone, come keep me company." And she'd pull me down the hall to her room, where we'd woozily recount the highlights like biblical lore, so buzzed off the night we were oblivious to our own exhaustion. She'd blast the Velvet Underground—her declared favorite—from the Crosley turntable and we'd dance to the sounds of Nico's apathetic drawl and Lou Reed's strung-out strums, performing for the security cameras all night long until our muscles gave in and we'd collapse onto her bed, where she'd trace the lines on my palm, pretending she could read them, or she'd have me massage her back with her kyanite crystal Reiki wand, asking me to press harder and deeper, saying don't hold back, stop holding back, don't be afraid to hurt me, so eventually I'd do as she said, and found that making Eva-Kate whimper in pain could be almost as gratifying as making her smile. Sleep would sneak up on us abruptly so that the next morning we'd wake in odd positions, as relics from the night, and laugh.

✹ ✹ ✹

One night was different than all the rest. A Wednesday. Five and six o'clock went by without Eva-Kate bursting through my door. I started drinking at seven to take the edge off my growing anxiety—a tall glass of whiskey with a splash of Coke. Then another. I thought about going over to her room, but was that what Mystery Friend would do? Dark Influence? What about Whiplash Girl Child? I didn't think so. So I scrolled through IKWYDLN, awestruck and giddy over the dozens of pictures of me with Eva-Kate. Me with Eva-Kate dancing under a broken disco light, me with Eva-Kate sharing an oversized tuft of cotton candy, me with Eva-Kate laughing on the rubberized floor of a bouncy castle, me and Eva-Kate in the Roosevelt Hotel pool wearing matching neon bikinis, me and Eva-Kate posing with various Jenners and Kardashians, me and Eva-Kate posing with Ashley Olsen, me and Eva-Kate posing with Jennifer Lawrence, me and Eva-Kate posing with Miley Cyrus, me and Eva-Kate posing with Nick Jonas, me and Eva-Kate posing with a six-foot-tall inflatable Furby made from Mylar and ripstop nylon. I looked good in the all-consuming light of a flashbulb, and the best part of it all was that Eva-Kate's entourage trinity—Josie, London, Olivia— were hardly there at all. It was like they'd been replaced. By me.

It was eleven by the time Eva-Kate showed up at my door, and she wasn't buzzing with her usual jumbled plans, or buzzing at all. She was pensive and downcast.

"Hey," she said, leaning her head against the doorway, "do you mind if we stay in tonight? I'm just not feeling it."

"Of course," I said from my horizontal position on the bed. "I don't care what we do."

"Wanna hang in my room? I'll make drinks."

"Obviously," I said, swinging my legs off the side of the bed.

"You da best, babycakes," she said, blowing me a lazy kiss.

Eva-Kate's room was rustic chic, distressed hardwood floors with a cowhide rug, exposed brick walls decorated with black-and-white photography, a silk gauze canopy hanging over an iron-framed bed.

"Before I forget," she said, getting onto her knees and reaching under the bed. She pulled out two packages, both with my name on them. "These came for you. I don't know what's in them but they're from Hot Toxic, so it's probably hair dye."

"Why would they send me hair dye?" I got down on the floor next to her to examine the shipping labels, make sure I wasn't hallucinating my name printed out in bold caps lock.

"They want you to be their Instagram spokesperson," she said. Hands-free, she got back onto her feet and closed the door.

"Wait, what?" This made more sense as a hallucination, so I was inclined to believe it was. "Why would they want me as their spokesperson? You're the one with dyed hair. I mean, *you're the one with the following.* This doesn't seem real." I wondered if she could tell I meant this literally, that I was actually insecure about the nature of our current reality.

"Course it's real. I didn't want to do it, so I said you would. You have like a hundred thousand followers now, you were gonna start getting hounded for sponsored posts soon anyway. You don't mind, do you?" She moved to the dresser, lighting a line of lavender-scented candles.

"*Mind?* No, I'm . . . I'm kind of speechless."

"Well, don't get too excited, they'll probably just pay like two thousand for a post since you're kinda new or whatever."

"*Two thousand dollars?* Are you serious?" I took a deep breath and tried to control my elation. In my sixteen years on Earth I'd made a total of five hundred dollars, money I'd scraped together from babysitting and birthday cards sent by relatives I'd never met. "Two thousand dollars is more than enough for me." I smiled graciously, keeping myself from bursting into ecstatic laughter by visualizing what my childhood rabbit looked like three days after she died. This always worked when I had to fight laughter or manufacture my most somber face.

"That's cute," she said in earnest. And then, with a gentle stroke of sadness in her voice, "I'm happy for you."

"Are you okay?" I asked as she slowly made her way to the antique bar cart on the other side of the room.

"Honestly? Not really." She took out two glasses and filled them halfway with Lagavulin 16.

"What's going on?"

"Nothing is working." She measured out two table-spoons of grenadine and dumped one into each glass. "The crystals, the hypnosis, the Reiki, the feather work, none of it. I'm still heartsick."

"Over Rob?"

"Sure, yeah." She poured a small splash of seltzer into the glasses and screwed the caps back onto their respective bottles. "But it's so much more than that. It's my life, it's just so . . . sad. Was I really put on this planet to be a pretty puppet for the masses to speculate about? They all think they know me, but the joke's on them because they can't possibly know me if I don't even know myself." She handed me my glass and clinked hers against mine. "Cheers, babycakes. Tell me if you like it, it's my own version of the Irish redhead. I don't use Sprite so it's mostly whiskey and grenadine. When I die they'll call it the Eva-Kate." The drink was deep magenta red and looked slippery in the glass. She sat down on the bed next to me.

"Cheers," I said, and dove into my drink. "You know, I don't think you need to know who you are. I don't think anybody really does."

"It's different for me." She shook her head. "It's not just that I don't know who I am, it's that I don't even know *if* I am. You know, I was fine before, I wasn't all morbid and existential until Rob broke things off and went after my sister."

She leaned her head back onto the wall so that all I could see was the white pillar of her exposed neck, the vague veins and vessels that swirled through like marble.

"That would make anybody existential and morbid,"

I told her. "This drink is dope, by the way. Way better than the bottled ones."

"This is a good batch," she agreed. "It's all about the proportions. In another life I was a Prohibition-era bartender. Or, like, one of those beautiful hostess women. I wish I was in this life, actually."

"You wish you were a hostess? Like *Liza*?"

"Just another one of the many ways she's hijacked my life."

"Don't you think you're a little bit too good for that? And by a little too good, I mean majorly and dramatically too good."

"You mean because I'm a celebrity? Sad to say that doesn't make me too good for anything. And if I had a down-to-earth blue-collar type job like a hostess, then people would respect me. I'd be one of the people, a *real* girl."

There was that *real girl* fantasy again. What did it mean for Eva-Kate?

"I'm sorry, I have to laugh." I was charmed by the fact that a hostess was her idea of a respectable blue-collar job. "You think hostesses get more respect than you do? You're a TV star, Eva-Kate, the whole country respects you."

"They don't. They think I'm this dumb, talentless child star who never deserved fame in the first place."

"They do not," I protested.

"Oh yeah?" She took out her phone and opened

Instagram, then handed the phone to me. "Just scroll through the comments. Take your time."

I couldn't believe what I was reading. I didn't want to see these horrible things people were writing, but I also couldn't look away:

> **@MiMiKaye:** You think you're so pretty but you're legit #forgettable.

> **@JonesSoJones:** Ew. My cat is a better actress than this wannabe.

> **@Freestyle4miles:** Eva-Kate Kelly should probably be dead. The world would be a better place.

> **@Billybob_Dylan:** Eva-Kate Kelly is an actual whore. I hope she chokes on a dick and dies.

> **@Lisa_Martina:** What a sick excuse for a female role model. I swear this girl has bubble gum for brains. And she thinks she's this smart, interesting activist or something—shut up, bitch, no one cares what you think!

> **@MaddieMad:** Haha look how much weight she gained! So fat now. That's karma for just overall sucking.

@ZephyrBitch: How ironic that EKK was the poster girl for ending teenage suicide, when she's the one who should actually kill herself.

@Robin6060: Eva-Kate Kelly doesn't deserve to be alive.

@Honey_SugarSugar: Eva-Kate Kelly should die, am I right? Talentless loser. LOL.

@THEXtinaFox: Does anyone else think this whore has a pig nose? Lmfao.

@ChillinVillin: It's not that she's even that bad of an actress, sometimes I think she's actually kind of good? But the thing is her face and her personality are so annoying they make me want to gouge her eyes out. Or my own eyes out. Or both.

@Katy.Kat2012: Why do all the good celebrities die while ppl like Eva-Kate Kelly get to live?

@These_prohibited_pieces: I hope you die, ya Barbie.

"This is awful." I passed the phone back to her. "Some people are so . . ."

"Pathetic. Sad. Desperate losers."

"I don't know how you deal with it."

"I barely can. The effort it takes to keep shaking it off is just . . ." She popped her eyes and let out an exasperated whistle. "Sometimes I think it could kill me."

"It would kill me." I nodded vehemently. "You're so strong."

"Eh." She shrugged off the compliment. "I don't know about that. I remind myself that haters are a quality problem, even a luxury. I try to think of them as accessories."

"That's brilliant."

"How've you been dealing with it, by the way? The Insta trolls. Surely you're acquiring some."

"I don't look. I can't."

"Then you're much smarter than I am. And stronger. Just like I suspected."

"You could ignore them too."

"Sometimes I think I'm addicted. Sometimes hate can feel like love."

"Well, *I* don't know how anyone could hate you."

"They don't really hate *me*, I've had to learn that over the years. They hate themselves and they project that onto me. Some of them are jealous. Some of them are just lonely. A lot of them don't see me as a real person, they think I'm larger than life, untouchable, so I couldn't possibly be hurt by what they say."

"But you are hurt. You're . . ."

"It's not even them I care about, they're idiots, they don't know me. I care about the people who know me, the people closest to me. It's their respect that I want."

"But don't you have that?"

"HA!" She threw her head back like it was the most absurd thing she'd heard in her whole life. "Of course I don't. My entire family hates me, and I hate them. My friends are only my friends because they think hanging around me is good for their careers, but soon they're gonna realize they're wrong. They're gonna realize I'm falling off the radar and they'll disappear. Rob realized it and look what happened to him. Someone told him it wasn't good for his image to keep dating a starlet famous for some dumb sitcom that no one even liked—"

"Oh please, everyone loved *Jennie and Jenny.*"

"Sure." She finished off her drink. "The moronic masses did, they'll eat that shit up. Don't know any better. But the critics, anyone who really matters, they all know *Jennie and Jenny* was trash. Sugary, overlit, oversaturated trash. And what have I done since then? Nothing. The fans are waiting for a second act. My managers tell me if I don't have my second act soon, the world will lose interest. They'll forget about me. I'll be a fixture of the past."

"That's not true! You were in *Summer Solstice* . . . you were nominated for a People's Choice Award. And then you did that other movie, uh, the remake of . . . was it *The Breakfast Club*?"

"It was *Pretty in Pink* and it practically ruined me. Nobody saw it. The PAs all leaked stories about me being a nightmare to work with. No one will hire me after that. So, what now? Modeling, music video appearances. Party appearances. Nothing to take seriously. I'm uneducated, homeschooling was a total joke. The last *book* I read was Lauren Conrad's autobiography. And I didn't even finish it. I have no talents. I'm not special. I'm just a child star burning out. This is *not* the second act they're expecting from me." She got up and went to pour herself another drink.

"That's absurd. But even if it were true, you're a human being, you don't have to be . . . entertainment. You don't have to be impressive. You can just be you."

"But that's the thing." She looked scared then, carrying her glass back to bed and bringing the whiskey bottle along. "I don't think I have a 'me.' Not anymore."

"What does that mea—"

"I've been Eva-Kate for so long, this persona, this character, this . . . *doll*, that I can't find the real me. She got lost under all this plastic. I buried her, and I don't think I can dig her out."

"Okay." I sat very still to try to counter her spiraling. "I know that's not true. You're being too hard on yourself. Let's . . ." I laced my fingers together and shifted my weight back and forth the way my mom always did when she was about to give an unsolicited psychological analysis. "Let's figure this out. Who . . ." I was timid but driven by a fierce curiosity. "Who is the real you? Who is the buried girl?"

"You sound like such a therapist," she said solemnly, looking up at the ceiling, then back at me. "Evelyn Kathleen. That's who I was before the auditions and the beauty pageants. We were Evelyn Kathleen and Elizabeth Jane McKelvoy. Then Liza quit and almost ruined my whole fucking life. But she didn't, and that's when I decided I was going to be a star. And if I was going to be a star, I couldn't be Evelyn Kathleen McKelvoy. I had to have a star's name. I had to be Eva-Kate Kelly."

"And what was Evelyn like? What are the qualities you buried with her?"

"I don't know," she snapped. "She was only seven. I have no real memories of her, it's like she never was. I've been a fantasy of a person for literally as long as I can remem—do you know the song 'Fake Plastic Trees' by Radiohead?"

I nodded, trying to recall the lyrics.

"That's me," she said. "Especially the third verse. The third verse has always made me so sad. Because that's all I am."

She looked at me expectantly, like I should know the third verse and be consoling her by this point, telling her it wasn't true.

"I . . . how does the third verse go?" I asked finally.

Eva-Kate closed her eyes and sighed.

"*She looks like the real thing, she tastes like the real thing, my fake plastic love.*"

"Oh."

"I *seem* real, I can make you *think* I'm real, but I'm just a fake plastic girl. And that's why Rob can't love me. He craves the real deal and he always will. Someone with a pulse, not some fraudulent human his agent hitched him to."

"Can I be honest? I'm so sick of this 'real' bullshit. Why do guys get to decide what it means to be a real girl? No one can tell you you're not real. That's not right."

"People should have substance," she lamented, ignoring what I'd said. "People shouldn't improvise who they are from moment to moment. Rob said Liza is honest about herself, unafraid to be herself, he says I am the way I am out of cowardice. He says I'm too empty to love."

"Then he's an idiot," I said, feeling my cheeks get hot. I hated that she made him a god in her mind when he didn't deserve even a fraction of her. "He's blind and ungrateful, and if he really thinks you're a fake plastic girl, then he doesn't get it. He doesn't know you." It felt good to hate him, it made it easy to believe everything he'd said outside the Roosevelt was bullshit. *He has it all wrong; he doesn't understand who she really is.*

"But you do?" she said, more curious than irked. She

reached again for the Lagavulin and poured what was left of it into her glass, then got to work emptying the glass.

"No—I don't know. I know you enough to know you're a living human girl at your core whether other people see it or not. I don't buy this plastic story you're telling yourself. Evelyn exists even if you've only been letting people see Eva-Kate."

"Maybe."

"And who is Rob to say what you are? I'm so sick of guys thinking they can define us with one word. Like, am I supposed to be flattered when a guy tells me I'm a 'tough' girl or a 'real' girl, as if the other girls he knows are weak and fake? It's just a way for them to feel powerful by pitting us against each other, and then against ourselves. And guess what?" The alcohol was alchemizing into liquid courage. I spoke with more conviction. "There are no such things as basic bitches. Only bitches you haven't gotten to know yet."

She thought this over quietly with a stone-cold stare, then broke into a giggle.

"Ruby says I can cast a spell to make him love me. I tried it but it didn't do anything. Of course." She rolled her eyes. "Don't ever tell anyone I even entertained the idea, it's beyond embarrassing."

"You know I wouldn't." If she had heard any of what I said, it was water off a duck's back now.

"Do you want to see it?"

"See what?"

"The love spell Ruby taught me."

"Oh. Sure." I didn't want to see the spell. I had a sinking feeling that something bad would happen if I did. If I tallied everything I'd had to drink that day, it added up to too much and I was getting a little dizzy, realizing I'd forgotten to eat.

"Naw." She smiled slyly. "Only if you really want to."

"I really want to," I said.

"Yay!" She sprang up and dragged a footstool to her bookshelf, then stepped onto it, barefoot and on tippy toes. She reached for items one by one and stored them in the crook of her elbow, then hopped down and brought them back to where we were sitting, hiding them dramatically behind her back.

"These are the ritual gloves," she said, slipping her hands into two supple leather gloves. "And thiiiiis is the crystal ball," she said in a mock-spooky voice, producing a transparent sphere about the size of a Magic 8 Ball and placing it onto the white duvet. It sank into the fabric, making a deep crater.

"Here we have . . . ," she announced, setting down a gold-plated wine goblet, "the chalice!" She took out a ziplock bag of salt from the goblet and set it to the side.

"It's . . . pretty," I said, noticing a hint of rust forming along the rim.

"And last but so very not least . . . drumroll, please . . .

badum-ch! The athame!" From behind her back she whipped out a five-inch dagger and grinned wildly at it. The handle was painted white with tiny cornflowers and tied with a green tulle bow. "Oooooooh," she cooed, waving it around like a wand, "so shiny."

"What's that for?" I asked, leaning away. She had a loose grip on the handle and I didn't want to be an accidental casualty.

"For blood!" She licked her lips.

"Wait, seriously? Whose?"

"No, not seriously. I'm just kidding. It's for, like, direction or . . . symbolism . . . I don't really know."

"But it's part of the spell?"

"I think so." She squinted at the sacred objects laid out on the bed, then at the athame, then back at the objects. "There's a sliiiight chance I may have forgotten how to do this."

"You don't have to," I told her, relieved, wanting to see her safely tucked into bed and for this day to be over. "Let's go to slee—"

"Blood of a lamb!" she recalled excitedly. "No matter the spell, my mom always used blood of a lamb."

"Your mom?"

"My mom is a practicing witch. The bad kind. Once upon a time, this athame was hers. Wasn't hard to get emancipated after I could prove *that*. Little-known fact: She got Liza into it too. They're both all about their rituals and enchantments and curses. Much darker shit than love spells. Here, hold it, feels really empowering."

"Okay . . . but you just said you were joking about the blood." I let her take my hands and guide them around the handle.

"Did I?" She kept her hands wrapped around mine and held them there.

"Uh, yeah. You did."

"Weird." She bit her bottom lip. "I must have meant human blood. The coven never used human blood—at least that I know of—but there was *definitely* lamb blood. Lots and lots of lamb blood." She giggled uncomfortably and sighed, drifting into the memory.

"No," I snapped then, pulling my hands out of her grasp so that the dagger fell to the bed. "This is ridiculous. I can't listen to this anymore. You don't need spells, okay? You're . . . you're completely perfect as you are, and if Rob doesn't see that, I swear to God he's—"

"You think I'm perfect?"

"You know what, yeah, I do." I was wasted. She was too. I hoped too wasted to remember any of what I was about to say, because once I'd started it felt like a crime to stop. "I think you're from another dimension. I think you're light-years too good for Rob and he doesn't deserve to date one fraction of you let alone all of you. I don't think you're a fake plastic girl, I think you're the realest girl I've ever met, and anybody who thinks you're fake just can't handle the fact that your spirit is . . . larger than life. Those people want the girl next door but you're so much more than that."

"Oh my God," she whispered, completely stunned, reaching for my cheeks and stroking them lightly, fingertips just barely touching my skin. "You understand me. You're the only person who—" She leaned in and pressed her lips to mine, kissing me desperately. I stiffened and held on to her hands, which had moved down to my collarbones.

"Eva-Kate, we're really drunk," I said as gently and steadily as I could.

"Doesn't matter." She shook her head. "You understand me and I need to show you how much that means to me. If I were sober I'd want the same thing. Promise." She looked me directly in the eye without blinking and I knew she was telling the truth.

"Okay," I acquiesced, letting her kiss me again, this time slipping her hands under my dress.

"Justine," she whispered, "I'm gonna give them a second act they never forget."

"I know that," I said, shivering. Her hands were cold as metal, just like the blade of her athame. "You don't have to prove yourself."

"Wait." She pulled away and a light went on in her eyes as if she'd just returned into her body. "Have you done this before? Have you ever been with a girl?"

"No . . ." I wiped the back of my hand against my mouth and sat back, embarrassed. "I've never been with—"

"You've never been with *anyone*," she remembered. "That's *right*. I'm sorry, that was dumb to even ask."

"It's okay, I don't mind." I shrugged and kept my shoulders lifted, too tense to know what to do with myself. "Have . . . you? Been with a girl."

"Tons of times." She put her hands on my cheeks, then moved them down so that they cupped my jawbone. "But always just for fun. Not like this."

I couldn't ask what she meant by *not like this* because she was kissing me again and I wanted so much more to kiss her than to ask any questions.

She tasted like grenadine and her lips were softer than seemed possible or human, as if the tiniest bite would cut right through, unraveling spools of tightly wound silk, leaving the toothy socket of her mouth open and exposed. So I was gentle. And passive. I let her take the lead and played the role of the first timer, the shy but open-minded student, obediently taking whispered directions, making my body lithe and pliable to her brazen hands.

As an actress herself, I wondered if she could tell I was acting. And if acting was a form of lying, could she tell that I was lying? The truth was, I had been with a girl before. Many times. And it was something I'd never told anyone. Her name was Annabel, and her room was on the same floor as mine at Bellflower. Long black hair, dark, frightened eyes. At just fourteen she was bipolar and paranoid, convinced the government was controlling us through chemicals they put in our food. At night when the nurses switched shifts, there was a brief moment when no one was keeping guard. We were expected to be in bed with the lights out, but Annabel used this narrow window of time to slip into my room, nimble and evanescent as a black cat in the night. She wasn't gentle with me, so I wasn't gentle with her. We clawed at each other, wanting our clipped nails to leave a mark, both of us trying to help the other feel something. We bit each other's lips hard, drawing blood. We slapped each other's faces, gripped our hands around each other's necks, all of it without making a sound. Getting caught was one thing we couldn't risk. And for this reason we never took our clothes off. A nurse could help herself to our unlocked door at any moment, and we had to be prepared.

So, when Eva-Kate lifted my dress up over my head, she became the first person to see me naked. Every muscle in my body cringed with an awful blend of dread and exhilaration. My mind wanted me to hide, but my body needed to be seen, and I hated it for that. Without her clothes on, Eva-Kate was a goddess cut from marble, and beside her, underneath her, I felt too real, more real than I'd ever wanted to believe. Inescapably real and crazy-stupid vulnerable. With Eva-Kate's body so fresh and current and tangible, the memory of Annabel felt tenuous, even false. I'd never told anybody about her, and she'd been dead for . . . What was it, three years? A painful lump formed in my throat when I realized I might never be able to prove to myself that she'd existed. I worried that when I fell asleep, this night with Eva-Kate would fade into the past and also become impossible to prove. I watched her fall asleep and then stared into the burgundy void of her canopy, willing my eyes to stay open, my eyelids heavy as two anvils. It became a competition, me against sleep. I thought as long as I kept my eyes open I could stay awake forever and set this moment as the new default present, safe from the smoke and mirrors of memory. But even with eyelids forced open, sleep snuck up behind me like a tidal wave and pulled me under.

CHAPTER 16

SEX AND CANDY

I woke up disoriented and alone, the vague evidence of
Eva-Kate in the wrinkled linen by my side. Her red
velvet curtains were thick and impenetrable, but nonetheless a searing beam of light cut through the tiny sliver
between them, so bright I had to shield my eyes. Blaring
music rattled the floor. It was coming from downstairs.

Beneath my blanket I saw that I was naked and gasped
so sharply it hurt my chest. The idea of me being naked
in somebody else's bed was so absurd it scared me. In an
instant, the fear transmuted to this vast, grand sadness
like a slimy gray liquid circling my heart. I didn't understand it. I thought I should be happy. Instead I had this
feeling like I'd taken something I didn't deserve.

I put on my dress and it felt like somebody else's

dress. My feet felt like somebody else's feet walking down the cold hardwood stairs. The air was freezing; she must have had the air-conditioning set somewhere around sixty-one. She liked it that way. *Frigid*, she'd said. *I want it so cold my teeth chatter.*

Out in the hallway, Eva-Kate's clear plastic landline was trilling. A pink light flashed on and off from inside the mechanism like a tiny heart on high alert. Tempted to answer it, I stopped myself and hurried on. I followed the thumping drumbeat and found her in the kitchen making French press coffee wearing nothing but heather-gray boy shorts. She was singing along to the music, "Never Let You Go" by Third Eye Blind, tapping her fingers against the counter as if it were a piano and she was playing the melody.

"Eeeeeeeh!" she squealed when she saw me, performing a professional-level pirouette without a hint of effort. "You're awake!" She had to scream so I could hear her over the music. I didn't know how I was supposed to behave after what happened. Had things changed? Was I supposed to kiss her? Tell her she looked beautiful? I wanted to do both, but her flighty insouciance made me second-guess whether anything really did happen.

"Your phone was ringing upstairs," I said. "The landline."

"Oh, that's fine." She shrugged it off. "Sit, sit. Coffee's almost ready."

I sat across from her on one of the bar stools that surrounded the marble island and laced my fingers together, insecure about what to do with my hands.

She tilted her face up and yelled into the air.

"LOWER MUSIC!"

"Lowering music," a smooth female voice replied, taking the volume down to a more reasonable decibel.

"So, how'd ya sleep?" she asked with a singsong lilt, snatching a cotton T-shirt off one of the bar stools and shimmying it over her head.

"I don't know," I said honestly. "Good, I think. How about you?"

I had woken up disoriented, a sure sign, when I thought about it, that I had descended deep down into the gorgeously inaccessible crypts of my subconscious.

"Cream? Sugar?" she asked, ignoring the question and pouring tar-brown liquid into two hammered-copper mugs.

"Oh . . . neither. Black is fine."

She wrinkled her nose.

"That's brutal," she said. "Do you hate yourself?"

"No!" I laughed. *Although, maybe*, I thought. "What's wrong with black coffee?" It's how Riley had been drinking it since middle school, getting off-the-walls wired before first period while the rest of us stared into space like zombies.

"Um, it's disgusting and you deserve better," she said,

pouring a generous stream of half-and-half into my mug. "Here, try this."

The cream swirled in hypnotic tendrils and rivulets through the steaming-hot black, too precious to drink. I waited for the clouds to dissolve then took a sip.

"Mmm, good, sweet," I said, though it was still too hot to taste. The song ended and was followed by "Sex and Candy" by Marcy Playground. I'd never heard it before, but the names of the songs appeared conveyed in blue on the sound system.

"Goddamn, I'll never get over this song," she said, taking a big gulp from her mug, eyes lighting up with sweetness. "This is my *jam*."

"I've never heard it," I admitted. I was gradually learning to let myself be imperfect around her. It was better than pretending to know everything and then fumbling to keep up the act.

"What?" She raised an eyebrow in disbelief. "How is that possible?"

"Is it . . . when did it come out?"

"*When did it come out?* Oh my God, you're seriously the cutest. It's from 1997. It was like a thing at the time, but people have forgotten it so hard it's like it never existed."

"How do *you* know it, then?"

"Oh," she sighed, looking down into the mug. "It was the last song on *Now That's What I Call Music*. You know what *that* is, don't you?"

"Yeah . . . there's like dozens of them, right?"

"Yeah, but this was the first one. It was in England before, but this was the first one to be released in America. It had some real nineties gems. Janet Jackson and the Spice Girls and Lenny Kravitz . . . oh my God, *Aqua*. Do you remember Aqua?"

"No!" I laughed, "Because I wasn't alive in the nineties! And neither were you."

"No, but my mom was obsessed with the music," she said with some sourness. "Anything from *any* part of the nineties . . . Nirvana, Backstreet Boys, didn't matter to her, she loved it all. She was really young when she had me and Liza, so this was the music from her childhood, her comfort music. And she played it all. Day. Long. So it became my comfort music too. Now listening to it makes me feel safe; you know that warm nostalgic feeling like being wrapped in a cashmere blanket?"

"Absolutely," I said, "I get that."

"Which is weird, though, because my mom is a sadistic psycho, so you'd think nineties jams would make me blue." She twisted her mouth into an amusedly puzzled knot and tapped one finger against her bottom lip as if she had a fun riddle to solve. "But it just doesn't. Nineties and early 2000s, man, I'm tellin' ya. One day civilization will look back and *know* that it was the true golden era."

"How was your mom a sadistic psycho?" I'd barely heard the rest of what she'd said after those two words.

These were bone-chilling words, but she'd rattled them off without hesitating or looking back.

"It doesn't really matter," she sighed, her energy taking a visible dive. "But the short version is that she didn't want kids. She was a pill-popping waitress who moved to LA for all the reasons people move to LA. Stupid reasons. Her boyfriend was a married man who ghosted when he heard she was pregnant. So she was bitter about the whole thing before we were even born. And I don't blame her for that part; getting knocked up and abandoned like that is fucked up."

"Awful," I agreed. Suddenly it felt like we were bartender and customer drinking over our blues in a dark dive bar, the extra grim kind with motorcyclists in leather loitering just outside.

"But so, fine, hate the asshole who did this to you, don't hate your babies. It's not their fault. They didn't ask for any of this."

"She didn't *hate* you." I laughed nervously. "Did she? Did she actually hate you?"

"Well, I don't really know what she was like before we were born, but when she had us, something went very, very wrong in her brain. She had this . . . delusion." Eva-Kate laughed the laugh of someone gearing up to speak the unbelievable. "I can't believe I'm saying this out loud. She had this delusion that Liza and I were God and the Devil incarnate. That's what she saw when she looked at us. I'm telling you, this woman was *wacko*. To her, Liza was God on Earth, an actual angel, and then I was the opposite . . . the weirdest part is that she's not even Christian."

"*That's* the weirdest part?" was all I could think to say.

"Sometimes I wonder how things would be if her visions had been reversed. If she'd seen pure goodness in me, would I be out there right now living some admirably average life like Liza gets to? Or did she see bad in me because I was born bad? Which came first, you know? Am I bad because she told me I was bad, or did she tell me I was bad because she saw something in me that scared her?" She looped her hair around one finger and brought it close to her mouth like a security blanket. "My eyes. She said I was born with dead eyes. You don't think I have dead eyes, do you?"

"*What?*" I was outraged. "Your eyes are literally brilliant. Everyone knows that! And what does that even mean anyway, 'dead eyes'? You were a baby, what were your eyes supposed to look like?"

"I know, *right*?" Her voice plumped up with artificial intrigue like she'd just received a delicious gumdrop of fresh gossip. "They say parents are hard on their kids, but Mama McKelvoy took it to a whole new level. And she spent most of my money on hiring the best publicity team on planet Earth. Same people who went on to cover up the Taylor Swift–Conor Kennedy car crash."

"Wow." I gawked, briefly impressed. "I can't even

imagine that. I . . ." I wavered between wanting her to elaborate and fearing what she might reveal next.

"I mean, what can ya do, right? At least Liza turned out okay. Or, like I said, maybe it's not that she turned out okay, but that she was born okay, born the good seed. Destined to be sane and stable. Oh well." She shrugged. "I guess we'll never know."

"Wait, hold on, do you really think Liza turned out better than you did? She's a *hostess*. Do you know how much money she probably makes? Basically none. And—"

"It's not about the money," she sighed. "I'd trade my money for the . . . I don't know, the *simplicity* of her life. And the peace of mind she always seems to have."

"But . . ." I couldn't understand. What were simplicity and peace of mind compared to everything Eva-Kate had? I had given up on simplicity and peace of mind a long time ago. They sounded nice, but I realized they weren't worth the effort. "Okay, fine, so you want to make some changes. But you're a teenager with this talent and incredible success—that you're totally worthy of, by the way—and Liza's dating your ex-boyfriend? How good and 'stable' could she really be?"

"Well, according to Rob, *very*. You know what it is? It's that she hasn't been damaged by this fucked-up industry and Rob just adores that innocence. He *left me* for that innocence. What an idiot. Just because she hasn't been eroded by fame doesn't mean she's better than I am."

"Of course not."

"Whatever." She shivered. "They can be together for now. If it lasts too long for my liking I'll end it."

"What do you mean? How?"

She cupped her hand over her mouth.

"I shouldn't be smiling. It's not funny. Although it's kind of funny."

"What is?" I matched her smile so she'd know I wouldn't judge. "You can tell me."

"Okay." She glanced around the room with casual suspicion, then leaned her elbows on the counter. "Last year I caught him cheating on me with some fourteen-year-old girl from Campbell Hall."

"Ew, *what*? Isn't that illegal?"

"Well, no, because he wasn't eighteen yet. But hold on, I haven't gotten to the good part yet. Or, I mean, the bad part."

"Okay, sorry, continue."

"It turned out he got her pregnant."

"Shut up."

"No, seriously. And *how* do I find this out? She came to me and asked for help. She didn't know who to talk to, her parents would have killed her, for all I know *Rob* could have killed her. And thank God she came to me before the press found out, now *that* would have been the true embarrassment. For both of us."

"So what did you do?"

"What do you think? I gave her cash to get an abortion and then some more to never tell anybody what happened. Then I pretended like everything was fine. Maybe I should have broken up with him at that point, but honestly, who has the energy?"

"Okay . . ." It seemed logical enough. I figured it's what I would do too. "But what does this have to do with him and Liza?"

"If I really wanted to break them up, I'd just show her the texts between Rob and the girl. Liza would never be with a guy who slept with a fourteen-year-old"—she rolled her eyes—"plus she's got that whole anti-abortion thing going on."

"How do you have their texts?"

"I had the girl send me screenshots back when this happened. I told her I needed them as proof that it really was his baby. I had to make sure she wasn't just some girl looking for money."

"*And you kept them?*" This wasn't really the part that shocked me, but it was the only part I could easily wrap my mind around.

"*Of course* I did. I knew I'd need the ammunition one day. You gotta stay one step ahead of everyone else if you're gonna survive."

"Right," I agreed, trying not to think about the things Rob had said to me. *The world would be a better place without her.* I wanted to have never heard this. I didn't want to have to tell her, but what if having these texts was putting her in danger? Did he know she had them?

"What's wrong?" she asked. I wondered how she could tell.

"What? What do you mean?"

"You just got really weird. You, like, zoned out for a second."

"I did? Oh. Well, yeah . . ." She might shoot the messenger, but it would be a better fate than if she found out I'd hidden this from her. "I have no idea how to say this, so, um, okay, I'll just . . . Rob approached me at that party."

"Shocking," she deadpanned. "And?"

"He . . . well, he said something that kind of scared me."

"Yeah, what's that?"

"He said the world would be a better place without you," I blurted. "And now I'm wondering if that had something to do with all of this. Like, maybe he's worried you're going to release the texts?"

Her face fell. She went from smug to devastated so quickly it frightened me. For a moment I wished more than anything I'd ever wished for that I hadn't said it. But then she closed her eyes and smiled very softly.

"Thank you so much for telling me," she said. "Ruby was right. You're so trustworthy."

"Do you know what he meant by that?" I stammered,

foreseeing the damage I might have just caused. I couldn't see it, but I felt it in my stomach, sticky and weighted like molasses.

"Let's get away," she said, in lieu of an answer. "San Luis Obispo. We'll go Friday. I can't think straight in this city."

I agreed without hesitation. Though, in retrospect, I realize she never actually gave me the option not to. Just a few weeks ago, if you'd told me I'd be going on a trip with Eva-Kate Kelly, I would have dropped dead from blissful disbelief. This was the dream. But now that she'd told me her secret blackmail plan, I couldn't help but see Rob's accusations in an unflattering new light.

The world would be a better place without her.

She's not who you think she is.

She's a puppet. And *the puppeteer.*

She keeps her friends close, but she likes to keep her enemies even closer. You know what I mean?

CHAPTER 17

FIFTY SHADES
OF HAIR DYE

*B*ack in my room, I opened the box from Hot Toxic, filled with tubes of hair dye in every shade you could imagine. The options left absolutely nothing to be desired. Their holographic labels read CANDY APPLE, SCARLET, FUCHSIA, FOLLY, AMETHYST, MAGENTA, VIOLET, WINE, LAPIS, IRIS, CYAN, STONE, ROBIN'S EGG, VERDIGRIS, KELLY, MINT, CORAL, TANGELO, AMBER, SUNGLOW. And that was only the very beginning. After an hour of trying to pick one, I was on the verge of a full-blown existential crisis. Which shade was *Justine Childs*? Which shade was *the* Justine Childs? Which shade was *me*? Who *was* I? The more I asked, the less I knew. I'd have to bleach my hair if I wanted any of the color to show up. With a quiet flash of panic, I felt my essence living in the pigment and feared it getting stripped away.

Instinctively, I snatched Princess Leia up from the foot of the bed and held her close.

My phone rang and startled me half to death. It was my mom, and I almost answered it. That's how on edge I felt. There was a part of me that actually *wanted* to talk to my mom. I had to remind myself that the mom I wanted was not the mom I had, and that the mom I had would actually make this worse. I let it go to voice mail and kept Princess Leia tucked into the crook of my elbow as I lined the multi-shaded tubes up flat against the bed in ten rows of five spanning from red to violet.

"Gorgeous," I said out loud, satisfied now that a sense of order had been restored. I took a picture from above and filtered it twice, first with Fresh on the AirBrush app, then Amaro on Instagram, then hit POST. #HotToxic, #InLove, #ColorMeUp.

The more likes that flooded in, the better I felt. It was as though a drug had kicked in, each like bumping me up to a higher high. Two hundred, five hundred, nine hundred. It hit one thousand and stopped there. My buzz plateaued and threatened to fizz out. I scrolled hungrily through the comments, eager to stay up here where the fresh, clear, thin air was an inhospitable environment for my anxieties.

@Byrx.Z25: 😍

@Byrx.Z25: why isn't your fine face in this pic?

@X_Jane_X: Get it girl!! 🖤 🍌

@LanaBanana: What's it like to be friends with Eva-Kate? I would DIE to be you.

@These_prohibited_pieces: #InLove, huh? Taking it to the next level with Eva-Kate?

Wait, what? I stopped reading. What did "taking it to the next level" mean? And did someone know about what happened last night? Who could have known? We were the only people here.

My phone vibrated, this time barely appearing on my radar. It was a text from Riley:

I haven't heard from you in a really long time. I hope you're okay and safe. I don't know how to reach your mom either.

I clicked DELETE and immediately forgot the message ever existed. I didn't have the bandwidth to get into it with Riley. I had to pack a bag for San Luis Obispo and choose a hair color by the time Eva-Kate's colorist showed up at two thirty. I picked robin's-egg and stuffed it into a pocket in my sweater and held it dearly like an amulet.

Taking it to the next level? The question rattled around somewhere in the back of my mind. Was that what we were doing? I wanted to ask her but dreaded the answer, whatever it might be. *She probably forgot that anything happened*, I told myself. *Or maybe nothing even did.*

CHAPTER 18

RED VINES AND A CIGARETTE

*N*obody talks about how frequently Taylor Swift writes lyrics about cars. Most people aren't really listening to the lyrics, and when they are, they're not thinking about them. But I am. I hear her lyrics and have no choice but to contemplate them all, sifting through them to find meaning in patterns as if they contain clues to some cosmic truth only Taylor has access to, the source from which she gets her talent and courage and faith and immunity to haters and superhuman energy. I never find the clues, but I do develop overly involved theories and analyses of Taylor Swift lyrics. Mostly it's the cars I'm fixated with; they're everywhere.

1. In "Tim McGraw," Taylor's summer love

drives an unreliable pickup truck that often gets stuck on back roads at night.

2. In "Fearless," Taylor asks this love interest to drive slow until they run out of road, then she says she never wants to leave the passenger seat.

3. In "Fifteen," Taylor's first date is with a guy on the football team who very impressively has his own car.

4. In "You Belong with Me," Taylor's friend and secret crush drives to her house in the middle of the night.

5. In "Back to December," Taylor recalls watching her ex laughing from the passenger side.

6. In "Treacherous," Taylor notices headlights shining in the night, presumably on a car being driven by the treacherous love interest she knows she should avoid. But can't.

7. In "All Too Well," a boyfriend we've come to believe is Jake Gyllenhaal almost runs a

red light because he's busy looking over at Taylor.

8. In "Style," the headlights are turned off as Taylor and boyfriend embark on a long drive that has potential to end in "paradise" OR in total destruction.

9. And on *Reputation*, Taylor tells her most epic automobile story to date in "Getaway Car," in which she uses Bonnie and Clyde as an analogy for her escape from not one but two different relationships. In the second verse she hops into the passenger seat of a new man's car and essentially tells him to step on it.

A quick Google search will give you lists of Taylor's car references, but what you can't find is any talk of what all these lyrics have in common. They're all about male, reckless drivers and/or about Taylor's position as the passenger. Though most often it's both: Taylor in the passenger seat of a car being driven dangerously by a man. You can look again if you don't believe me, go ahead.

Why is she so drawn to men who drive like maniacs? I can't really know. Maybe it's the element of thrill and danger that makes her feel alive, a feeling she's lost touch with living up in her ivory tower. Second question: Why is she always in the passenger seat? Why, in her repeated use of car imagery, does she never take the wheel? Seems to me like, in spite of all her fame and fortune, Taylor Swift is still caged in by antiquated patriarchal values. But I'm not saying this in the "Taylor Swift isn't a feminist" way that everyone loves to do—she *is* a feminist, and I could argue that to the death—I'm just observing that the code of the patriarchy is so deeply entrenched in the collective unconscious that even an unstoppable powerhouse like Taylor Swift hasn't totally felt comfortable getting into the driver's seat of her own life.

✻ ✻ ✻

This is what I was thinking from the passenger seat of Eva-Kate's Audi as she rocketed us north on the 101 freeway, Princess Leia asleep and softly snoring on my lap. Josie sat in the back seat, looking vaguely hungover with her bedraggled brown hair hanging heavily over waxy-white cheeks. She had her spidery legs pulled into her chest and she wrapped her arms around them, typing vehemently on her new iPhone X. I tried to read her face from its reflection in the right-side mirror. It said something like nausea and resentment. I felt a little bit bad for her and worried I was taking her spot in the passenger seat. I wouldn't blame her for resenting me. But I also wasn't going to offer up my seat. I finally understood that I belonged there.

I swiveled my gaze to the side mirror and grinned

uncontrollably, my face possessed by the unfamiliar feeling of satisfaction. Seeing my new mermaid-blue hair blowing in the wind would never get old.

"Can we stop here for a minute?" Josie asked when we neared the exit to Solvang. "I need Red Vines and a cigarette."

"There are Red Vines under your seat and a spare pack of Parliaments in that console to your left," Eva-Kate said. "We're not stopping at those stupid fucking Danish windmills. I'm sick of redneck tourists telling me to go fuck myself whenever I won't pose for a photo."

CHAPTER 19

EMOTIONAL
SUPPORT GIRL

We made it to the Madonna Inn by 5:00 P.M., the sun still a painful, tingling blister in the sky. Eva-Kate sent Josie to get our keys, then pulled me in by my waist to take a selfie. I saw Josie roll her eyes at us before pulling open the door to the imitation Swiss chalet lobby and disappearing inside.

"She gets grumpy," Eva-Kate said, absently swiping through filters. "Forgets she literally begged me for this job."

I bent down to clip Princess Leia onto her leash and considered how to respond, but couldn't think of anything. I was getting grumpy too; three hours in the car without stopping had me starving and carsick, too lightheaded to know what I wanted, let alone how to ask for it.

"She'll be fine," I said, squinting into the glare of sun bouncing off an entire lot of windshields.

"Damn straight she will be," she agreed, surveying the cars as they drove into the lot. "Let's just hope she doesn't take too long. I'm carsick as fuck and need to be poolside ASAP."

A wind picked up, blowing through Eva-Kate's freshly flamingo-pink hair. She laughed, shaking the effulgent locks off her face, peeling away the strands that caught in her lipstick.

❉ ❉ ❉

Our room was in a pseudo-Swiss alpine chalet with heavy storybook vibes and 1980s kitsch. To get there we had to climb three flights of white wood doily-patterned spiral stairs to the very top, Josie carrying our bags the whole way. When I insisted on carrying my own, Eva-Kate put her hand against my cheek and said:

"Don't be ridiculous. You're my guest, and my guests don't carry luggage."

I made a point of avoiding the look on Josie's face then. I knew it would be devastating.

The rooms at the Madonna Inn have their own unique themes. Ours was "Just Heaven," a gaudy rendition of the afterlife decorated with French canopy chairs, golden cherub chandeliers, and white satin throw pillows looking like clouds on top of the baby-blue shag carpeting that climbed up a spiral staircase in the center of the room, leading to a stained glass spire with a view of the rolling hills of San Luis Obispo and the 101 freeway cutting through.

Josie's room was one floor beneath ours and called "Traveler's Yacht."

"You don't have to feel bad for her," Eva-Kate assured me once we were alone our room. "She likes having her own space. And besides, our room only has one bed, so where would she sleep, you know?"

"Sure." I nodded. But Eva-Kate had misread my energy. I didn't feel bad for Josie. I felt bad about not feeling bad for her.

✱ ✱ ✱

"I'm gonna need to see some ID," the poolside bartender said as soon as he saw us approaching. He was scrawny with uneven facial hair, like he could have been a teenager himself, and wore a tie-dyed T-shirt that read: *I'd rather be in San Luis Obispo.*

In LA we never had to use fake IDs, Eva-Kate knew all the bouncers (or they knew her), and I'd come to assume we could get in anywhere without batting an eyelash. Though if an eyelash had to be batted from time to time, Eva-Kate was more than happy to oblige.

"It would *be my pleasure*," Eva-Kate said then, opening her wallet and, with an easy flick of her wrist, produced two California driver's licenses with our faces on them. She held them out to him in a two-card fan, standing with the confidence of knowing she had a winning hand, but a face that would never give it away.

"Mary Martins and Scarlett Seyfried," he read from the IDs, tilting them back and forth, checking for their holographic seals. "What'll you be having?"

"A strawberry daiquiri for me." She accepted the cards back from him with a gracious smile. "And Scarlett over here will have the mojito."

"Also strawberry?" he asked.

"Also strawberry," she said, running the corner of her AmEx lightly against her bottom lip.

We drank our strawberry concoctions poolside as the sun set. A handful of patrons lounged on chairs around us or sat perched at the bar beneath a rotunda gazebo. Aside from the occasional brief double take, nobody paid us much attention, which was both a relief and a disappointment. I was beginning to develop a love/hate romance with being stared at by strangers.

"Stay right like that." Eva-Kate, in a string bikini and silk kimono robe, took out her phone and snapped a picture of me reclined in my chair, a wide-brimmed sun hat casting my eyes in shadow. "What a fucking *muse*," she raved, furiously typing out a caption. "You are the light *of my life*. And of my Instagram."

I smiled weakly, the compliment eclipsed by concern for what I looked like in the picture she was now broadcasting to her millions of followers. She'd put me in the same tiny bikini she had on, only I didn't have a robe to cover up. I sensed that I was dangerously exposed, and had to suck down as much of the fruity rum as I could to feel at ease in my skin.

Eva-Kate put her phone away and slipped herself onto my chair so that she was pressed up against me. My heart stopped so suddenly I almost wished she'd move away. I needed some tiny sliver of space between us to keep her electric magnetism from overpowering me. But I'd never tell her that. She had me caught her in tidal pull and the only thing I'd ever tell her was yes.

"I don't always have the best instincts," she said, running her hand up my thigh. It felt unreasonably, unbearably sublime, like a pixie planting a million kisses, sending shivers from head to toe. "But I am *such* a genius for bringing you here. Everything is so much better when you're next to me."

"Oh, stop." I had to laugh. Though she had me undeniably spellbound, her imperfections were glaring, and that saccharine use of hyperbole was a big one. "I know you don't mean that."

"What?" She looked hurt. "Of course I do!"

"Wait, actually?" I saw something strikingly genuine in her face and swallowed hard.

"Uh, yeah, actually." She smiled, our faces so close together I thought I could taste her lipstick. "Why else would I keep you around? You're my emotional support girl."

"I am *so* sorry to interrupt you!" A trio of twelve-year-olds appeared at our side, adorably jittery and blushing. The girl who spoke was the tallest of the group and wore a T-shirt with the Victoria's Secret PINK logo emblazoned in college font.

"Yes?" Eva-Kate smiled up at the girl but withheld her acceptance of the apology.

"We just wanted to say hi, and we're, umm, just, like—"

"We're huge fans and we love you!" another one of the girls blurted. She had on a silver one-piece and wore her rusty red hair in an endearingly neat ponytail.

"Clara!" the third one scolded. "You said you'd be cool."

"Oh, but she *is* cool," Eva-Kate assured them. "You *all* are. What are your names? I know this is Clara, and who are you two?"

"I'm Elise," said the tallest one, bursting with excitement. "And this is Jessica."

"*Jess*," the third friend corrected her giddily.

"Great to meet you." Eva-Kate took the time to shake their hands. "And this is my friend—"

"It's Justine!" Clara squealed, seeing my face beneath the hat.

"*Obvi*." Jess gripped Clara's arm and waved shyly at me.

"You . . . *you know who I am*?" I had to bite down hard on my lip to keep from drowning out their giddiness with my own.

"Are you joking?" Jess stared. "You're Justine Childs, everyone knows who you are."

"You have one hundred and twenty *thousand* followers," Clara informed me, making my list of top five favorite people of all time.

"We all love your new hair," said Elise. "Everyone is talking about it."

"OhmyGod, *no one* is going to believe we met them," Clara said to her friends.

"So true," Jess agreed. "Can you believe we almost didn't come down to the pool? This would have just never happened."

"Well, hey, why don't we get a pic together?" suggested Eva-Kate. "Then your friends will have to believe you, right?"

The girls glanced starry-eyed between one another like they couldn't fathom what they'd done to deserve such luck. The luck of being in our presence, not just Eva-Kate's but mine too. Elise ran back to their chairs to get her selfie stick and we huddled in together with me and Eva-Kate in the middle. Any insecurity I'd had about my bikini body vanished. I had fans. People who knew my name. People who wanted to take a picture with me. Sure, they were twelve-year-old girls, but twelve-year-old girls are the future.

This was all I'd ever wanted. And it felt fucking good.

CHAPTER 20

BABY'S FIRST PAYCHECK

W *hat the fuck is wrong with you, Justine?*

We were sitting at a pink pleather booth in the Madonna Inn restaurant for 1:00 P.M. breakfast when a text came through from Riley. This time I bit:

Excuse me? I typed back, half distracted by Eva-Kate and Josie, who I could see laughing out of the corner of my eye. The vague animosity between them seemed to have lifted. They were admiring the bedazzled hearts hanging from the ceiling and the tree trunks that grew through the room from floor to ceiling.

"It's like the Rainforest Cafe, but for love." Eva-Kate giggled, getting out her phone.

You haven't responded to any of my texts but I know you're getting them. I see you posting on Instagram. Why are you ignoring me?

I wrote back: *I'm not. I just need my space.*

Riley: *I got through to your mom. Your parents got divorced? And you didn't tell me? I don't get it, what the fuck is going on?*

A lump formed in my throat. I didn't like her throwing my own life in my face. That was my business and for me to regulate.

Me: *They didn't get divorced. They're GETTING divorced. It's a weird time and I need some space, okay?*

Riley: *No, it's not okay. Why do you think you can just cut your friends out on a whim without bothering to give an explanation? Don't you care at all about hurting people? Don't you think we deserve to at least hear why you won't return our calls or texts?*

Me: *Honestly, Riley, I don't know what you do or don't deserve, but I know it's not my job to explain myself to you. I don't owe that to you or anybody else.*

A few minutes went by and I had almost begun to believe that was the end of it. But she came back with one more text, always having to get the last word:

I've always suspected you never really cared about anyone other than yourself, but now I know it for sure. It's called sociopathy, Justine, you're a sociopath.

I flipped my phone facedown so I could begin the process of forgetting this ever happened. *You don't care what Riley thinks anyway,* I told myself. *She's never wanted you to be happy. That's why you stopped responding to her in the first place.*

"Justine, you okay?" Eva-Kate lifted my chin with her finger, drawing my eyes to hers.

"Yeah." I forced a smile. "Just a dumb text from an old friend. What did I miss?"

"We ordered enough cake to kill a small child," Josie boasted. She seemed to think this was something to be proud of, though I couldn't see how. "We'll never eat it all, but we absolutely one hundred percent need it for the photo op."

"They're called pink champagne cakes and they're like a foot tall, sprinkled with big sugar granules that look like diamonds."

"And you always think they're about to fall over but they never do."

"In the breakfast nook on the set of *Jennie* we had these pristine pancakes I used to absolutely drool over. They weren't real, they were just plastic, but my mind must have never really understood that, because I craved them anyway." She laughed at herself, then retreated into the memory. Though her eyes stayed open, they were glassy and blank. It was clear she had gone somewhere else entirely.

"She gets trance-y like this," Josie assured me. "It happens when she remembers shooting *Jennie and Jenny*. I think it's a happy place for her, she feels safe there."

I know that, I wanted to tell Josie, feeling possessive. *I've been living with her for over two weeks, remember?*

"I'm trance-y, not *in a trance.*" Eva-Kate blinked and took a big gulp of ice water from her chalice. "I can still hear you."

Our waitress appeared, balancing the towers of pink champagne cakes. They looked so amusingly cartoonish, and so did she in her traditional Swiss dress uniform with a white doily apron and her dirty-blond hair pulled up into tight Swiss braids on top of her head.

"Anything else I can do for you ladies?" she asked sweetly, with a slight southern twang, revealing a mouth of crowded teeth, one of the two in front chipped diagonally in half.

"Three Bellinis would be great, thanks." Eva-Kate batted her eyelashes and expertly handed the menus over to the waitress (name tag: Greta), who clutched them to her chest and frowned, saying:

"I'll have to see your IDs."

"Oh." Eva-Kate's face fell theatrically. "We didn't bring our wallets, I usually just charge breakfast to the room."

"Well—"

"I guess I could go all the way up the hill to get them. It probably wouldn't take more than ten or fifteen minutes to get there and back, and you guys don't mind waiting, right?" she asked us, making us perfect props for her performance. I didn't know if this was my cue to say anything or if like any good prop, I should stay quiet and still.

"Oh, please, don't be silly." She gave Eva-Kate a mischievous side smile. "Normally I'd have to insist, but there's no one else on duty and my friends would never forgive me if they found out I withheld Bellinis from Eva-Kate Kelly."

"Ha!" Eva-Kate laughed with her. "You've made my day, Greta, you sneaky angel. I hope you like inappropriately generous tips."

I thought the charm was just a bit over the top, but it was working on Greta. She brought us our Bellinis and the bill, then bowed her head thankfully and said:

"No rush, ladies, take your time."

I didn't like the Bellini; the peach puree was too thick and the sparkling wine bubbles fizzed up my nose, and I didn't like Riley calling me a sociopath. Was it sociopathic to want to take care of my own needs and not let negative energies drag me down? It was true, I had dropped her and the others without considering their feelings. But that was because none of them cared about my feelings either. Where had they been while I was in Bellflower? Riley came once and left after ten minutes when she saw the psychotic patients in the common room zoning out on Haldol. She never came back. And she says I'm the sociopath? I suspected this was one of her many mind games: make me feel like I needed to come back to her and apologize. But game or not, the suggestion wasn't sitting well with me. She wasn't the first person to use that *S* word on me, so I had to wonder: Were these people trying to gaslight me into believing in my own sociopathy and relinquishing my power to them, or were they telling me the truth they saw in me? Either way, it took away my appetite. I poked at my pink champagne cake and took tiny sips from my Bellini every time Eva-Kate looked in my direction. When those few sips added up to a buzz, I was able to down the rest of it without noticing the pulpy peach and sharp fizz as it slid down my throat.

"I want to make a toast." Eva-Kate raised her chalice. As the light shifted over it, I saw the glass was speckled with some kind of multicolored chrome powder. Josie and I raised ours in response.

"Here's to my real friends who let me know what people are saying behind my back. And that's you two, my real friends. No one else. So, cheers." She clunked her chalice hard against ours, throwing grace and elegance out the window.

Real friends. A few days ago I would have delighted in the promotion to Josie Bishop–level friendship status, but now it felt more like a demotion. That's the moment I knew I didn't want to just be her friend, no matter how "real."

"Is this about Rob? So what are you gonna do about it?" asked Josie. "Confront him?"

"Confront him? God no." Eva-Kate scowled, horrified

by the mere suggestion. "This is about keeping my reputation intact, Josie, not destroying it."

"So then what?"

"There's only one thing I *can* do." Eva-Kate shrugged. "Make him wish, for the rest of his life, that he'd never started talking shit in the first place. I can't make him love me, fine, but I can make him fear me."

"So . . ." Josie pressed, "what are you going to do?"

"Release the texts." She smiled slyly.

"Whoa," Josie said. "You're merciless."

"*On the contrary.*" Eva-Kate slammed her chalice down. "I've given him plenty of opportunities to be on my good side."

"What about the girl?" Josie asked. I stayed quiet. It sounded to me like Eva-Kate was asking for trouble, and I had a bad feeling about it.

"What about her?"

"If you release the texts, won't you be outing her too?"

Eva-Kate rolled her eyes. "I'm not gonna say her name."

"Still, you know the press will do everything they can to find out who she is and track her down."

"Well, maybe she should have considered that when she slept with my boyfriend," Eva-Kate snapped. "She's not my problem anymore."

I needed another drink. I glanced around for Greta the Waitress but didn't see her, so I picked up my phone as a quick distraction. A pattern disrupter.

There were ten new text messages from Riley. I deleted them in one swipe without thinking twice, then waited for my email to load.

"Oh my God." I clapped my hand to my mouth. A hot current surged through my body, "The Hot Toxic contract money came through."

Ten thousand dollars. I read the number over and over again, thinking it couldn't be real. It wasn't possible.

"Awwwww!" Eva-Kate caught me off guard with her lips suddenly pressed snugly against mine in an aggressively sensual kiss. "It's baby's first paycheck!"

I thought I could feel my eyes popping out of their sockets. I'd never had more than nine hundred dollars in my bank account at one time, and Eva-Kate had never kissed me in front of anybody like that before. But Josie was unruffled, as if she'd seen it all, including this, a million times.

"How much is it for?" she asked me point-blank, with the most tepid fake smile. I was disappointed. I'd wanted her to be shocked to see us kiss, I'd wanted her to be jealous and even a little threatened by my prominent role in Eva-Kate's life. Her blasé expression was anticlimactic. It would have killed the buzz if not for the ten thousand dollars I could practically feel burning a hole in my bank account.

"Nosy Josie!" Eva-Kate scolded, then said to me, "You don't have to tell her, you're better off keeping what you make to yourself. Trust me."

"I trust you."

"So, what are we gonna do to celebrate?" she asked. A starry glimmer in her eyes said she already had something in mind.

"I don't know . . ."

"You gotta go big or go home," Josie challenged me.

"I'm not going home," I replied, staring her steadily in the eye.

"That's my girl." Eva-Kate beamed. "Guess that means we're going big."

CHAPTER 21

LOST CAUSE

I'm coming home tomorrow. I tried to call you. Please call me back.

This text came in from my mom while I was curled up in the Audi's back seat, holding Princess Leia against my chest. I was carsick and had a splitting headache from whatever I had ingested the previous night.

I ignored her text, too sick to respond. I didn't want her to come home. I think a part of me was hoping she wouldn't come home at all. I prayed for sleep but it wouldn't take me.

Because I wanted to lie down in the back, Josie got to sit up front, resting her bare feet up on the dashboard.

"I'm so tired of feeling sick," she said despondently, as if it were a lost cause.

I wondered if she was a lost cause. What plans did she

have, what did she want from life other than escaping reality with Eva-Kate day in and day out? I wondered if Eva-Kate was a lost cause, and if entwining myself with her would make me a lost cause. My cause had been to assimilate myself with the rich and famous, and now I could hardly remember why. I had never been so exhausted in my entire life.

❈ ❈ ❈

Back at Eva-Kate's place, we found London and Olivia in the living room sprawled out on the cowskin rug, smoking cigarettes and laughing over a magazine.

"Jesus *fucking* Christ." Eva-Kate clutched her chest. "You scared me half to death. What the *fuck* are you doing here?"

I scooped Princess Leia up and slipped past Eva-Kate onto the stairs, hoping to extract myself from the confrontation that was no doubt about to happen.

"We heard about your little getaway," I heard London say. "Kinda hurtful that we weren't invited."

I paused on the fifth step so I could keep listening.

"Dammit, Josie, you *told* them?"

"No! I didn't, I swear."

"She didn't," Olivia confirmed. "We read it."

"You *read* it? *Where?*" Eva-Kate quizzed her skeptically. I didn't believe it either. *Who could have written about our trip? Who could have known we were there?*

"Perez Hilton," said London. "Obviously."

"Well who the fuck told him we were there? It's San Luis Obispo; someone had to tip him off."

"I dunno, but whoever it was took some great pics."

I turned to ice. *What had they seen?* I knew the answer. The answer was obvious and humiliating and terrifying.

R R R R R R R R R I I I I I I I I N N G G G G G G RRRRRRRIIIIIIINNGGGGGGGG!

The landline upstairs began to ring, the rattling so shrill and loud it sounded as though it was coming from inside my head.

"That's bullshit," Josie said. "I'm always on paparazzi lookout. You know I care more about Eva-Kate's image than even she does. No one was there."

"*Hey.*" I could imagine Olivia shrugging with fake nonchalance. "Don't shoot the messenger."

R R R R R R R R R I I I I I I I I N N G G G G G G RRRRRRRIIIIIIINNGGGGGGGG!

It went again, this time prompting Princess Leia to wriggle out of my arms and dash up the stairs, unclipped nails scratching at the wood. I put a hand over one of my ears so I could block out the stridence and still eavesdrop.

"She's bluffing," Eva-Kate reported smugly. "There's one picture on here and it's a faraway shot of me getting out of my car."

"But still," Josie said, "someone had to tell them we were there."

"Well, it wasn't Justine," said Eva-Kate. "She was with me the whole time. So, was it *you*?"

"Are you kidding me, Eva-Kate?" Josie snapped. "Me? Really?"

"Wanna tell me who else?"

R R R R R R R R R I I I I I I I I N N G G G G G G G RRRRRRRRIIIIIIINNGGGGGGGG!

Fuck this, I thought, heading up after Princess Leia. If there were no pictures of me after all, then I had no more to hear. I walked to the end of the hall, where the early nineties clear plastic landline sat perched on a misplaced dining room chair. I reached out to silence it, but just then, the answering machine picked up.

"Hey, it's Eva-Kate." Her voice came from the machine, hushed compared to the earsplitting ring. *"Thanks for calling my super rad landline. I'm not one hundred percent sure how to check these messages, but go ahead and leave one anyway after the beep."* BEEEEEEEEEEP.

There was no way I could have predicted what was about to happen next. And when it did happen, I thought—no, I *knew*—I had to be hallucinating. I *had* to be, because what I was hearing couldn't possibly be real.

CHAPTER 22

EVELYN KATHLEEN

"*H*i, Eva-Kate, this is Dr. Childs," the voice message began. "I'm calling to let you know I'll be back in Los Angeles next week, and will be available to resume our evening sessions on Tuesday. Looking forward to hearing from you, bye for now."

It was my mom's voice. Leaving a message for Eva-Kate. I stared at the clunky, outdated machine until my vision blurred as if waiting for it to tell me more. I pressed REWIND and listened again. And then again. *Our evening sessions*, she'd said, which meant something that just couldn't be true: My mom was Eva-Kate's therapist. *Why didn't Eva-Kate tell me? She had to have known, so why didn't she tell me?* I could feel sweat beading on my forehead because the realness of it all was starting to sink in. Each time I rewound the tape it became more and more clear that my mind was not playing tricks on me. Eva-Kate had known all along that my mom was her therapist and she'd kept it from me. I didn't know why, but I did know one thing for sure: People don't keep secrets when they have nothing to hide.

"Justine?" Eva-Kate spoke from behind me. "What are you doing over there?"

I turned around slowly. Suddenly, she was once again an absolute stranger to me. The weeks we'd spent together unraveled and I knew then in my gut that I'd missed something; somewhere along the line I'd overlooked what I'd never been too comfortable with: the truth.

"Tell me it's a coincidence," I pleaded.

"What are you talking about?" She laughed nervously, peeking over my shoulder to see the answering machine. The color in her face faded and she swallowed hard, then smiled to cover it up.

"Your therapist," I said, my voice timid and wavering. "You knew she was my mom. We have the same last name, we live in the same house, so you knew. Now I just need to know: Was it a coincidence, or did you . . ."

"Did I move across the street from my therapist on *purpose*?"

"You moved in right after she left for India," I thought out loud. "You knew she was leaving. Wait." I shook my head and put my hand out so she'd stay where she was.

"What am I thinking? There's no coincidence, that's not even possible. Her office is at our house, so when you bought this place you knew exactly what you were doing."

"Of course I knew where she lived; I'm not a moron."

"No, you're not, are you? You're smart. In your world everything is intentional, accidents don't happen."

"Justine"—she smiled gently—"you're being a little dramatic. My realtor showed me the house and I fell in love with it. It was a coincidence that it happened to be across from Dr. Childs's house. What was I gonna do, *not* buy the house just because my therapist lived nearby? It's really no big deal. I told her how much I loved the house, we talked it through and decided it wouldn't be too weird. And when you and I started hanging out, I didn't want to tell you because I thought you'd think I was like some weird stalker. I'm sorry, I should have told you."

I thought this over, repeated it back to myself.

"Oh," I said, pretending to be relieved, pretending to be embarrassed. I sighed heavily, let all the tension out of my shoulders, and laughed at myself. "Wow, Eva-Kate, I'm so sorry. I must still be all messed up from last night."

"Aw, babe, that's okay." She got closer and kissed me on the side of my mouth. I tried my best not to flinch. "Your serotonin is totally depleted right now. Mine is too. Come, let's sleep it off. I'd rather be unconscious anyway."

"There's literally nothing I'd rather do right now," I

told her, mustering every ounce of sincerity I had in me, "but Princess Leia's been cooped up for so long and I really need to take her on a walk. You go to sleep and when I get back I'll join you, okay?"

She agreed and slunk off to her room, effortlessly dexterous as a cat.

I grabbed Princess Leia from my room and walked downstairs as quickly as I could without letting on that I was rushing. When I walked through the front door and was standing outside, a wild shudder shook my body, because I *knew* my mom, and knew that if she'd even had the slightest idea that a teenage celebrity with Eva-Kate's reputation was moving in across the canal, she would have been calling daily to make sure I kept my distance. Eva-Kate hadn't told her. She'd bought the house and waited until she knew my mom was gone to move in. She'd known all along that I was the daughter of her therapist, but she never said anything, and she lied when I'd confronted her about it. I knew then that I'd been living in a lie, and as long as I stayed in that house, I'd never know the truth.

CHAPTER 23

TRANSFERENCE

I took the long way around the block to the back of my house so that nobody would see me. I found the key she kept in a hollow plastic rock and opened the French doors, then bolted them shut behind me. I closed the curtains and shut off the lights.

I looked around and realized I hadn't been in the office for a long time. Possibly years. A lot had changed. The furniture was now in an entirely green color scheme with abstract paintings of deciduous forests and a Zen garden, sand fully smoothed over, on top of a glass-top coffee table. Behind the couch was a wicker room divider, and behind that was my mom's desk. Her patients wouldn't be able to see it just by standing in the room; they would have had to slip past the couch and around to the other side of the divider, which itself was too tightly woven to see through.

Compared to the main portion of the room, the sequestered area was unruly, papers and pens and envelopes and clipboards and coffee mugs and vitamin bottles and pushpins and paper clips strewn about with absolutely no rhyme or reason. To the far right was a file cabinet sitting beneath a framed picture of me posing with Princess Leia just a month or so before Bellflower. My hair was in braids and I was wearing a loose-fitting red T-shirt with Taylor Swift's silk-screened face beneath the number 22. It's so cute, in that song, when she mentions the cool kids who've never heard of Taylor Swift. Maybe once upon a time there were cool kids who'd never heard of Taylor Swift, but I'd say ever since 2009, kids *that* cool were as fictional as unicorns. Okay, fine, so maybe Kanye *did* give her fame a boost.

Eva-Kate had said she'd introduce me, but never did. Among many other things, this would be the summer I almost met Taylor Swift but didn't.

"Oh my God," I gasped as the realization hit me: Eva-Kate had seen this picture. Not only had she known who my mom was from the day she met me, but she had actually known about *me* long before that.

I yanked at the file cabinet handle but it was locked tightly, no wiggle room whatsoever. I looked around for the keyhole but there was none. And even if there had been, did I have time to go searching for a key? I certainly didn't have the patience. Frustrated, I pulled again. This time, a high-pitched, squeaky-clean *beep beep beep beep* went off and wouldn't stop.

"Oh no." I put my hands flat on top of the cabinet, panicking just a little. "No, no, it's okay, shhhhhhhh, it's okay, I'm not . . . okay, Jesus, please stop, please stop."

Trying to figure out where the sound was coming from, I found a keypad on the right side of the steel box.

"Oh, thank God," I said. "Okay, let's see. Let's see."

The passcode to open the cabinet had to be a six-digit number combination. The beeping wouldn't stop until I got it right, so I had to work fast—what if the alarm was set up to alert my mom? Or worse, a home security company? They could show up at any minute. But I couldn't afford to think about that.

I typed in my birthday: 02-02-01.

Wrong. I tried her birthday, but it didn't work either. I knew it couldn't possibly be my dad's or Aunt Jillian's, but I tried those just in case. Wrong and wrong. Who else could there be? Or maybe it wasn't a birthday. I tried some other important dates—her wedding day, the day she moved to Los Angeles, the day they found the bungalow on Carroll Canal—but none of those were it either. The beeping got faster and faster; I was running out of time and my mind kept going back to birthdays. A sick feeling at the pit of my stomach was telling me the date I had to try next, but I couldn't bring myself to type it in. If it turned out to be right, there'd be no turning back from the mouth of the rabbit hole.

"You have ten seconds remaining." An outdated electronic voice spoke from the cabinet. "Countdown initiating. Ten, nine . . ."

"*Fuck*," I swore. "Ten seconds until *what*?" I thought maybe I should just run, forget about the files. The home security team might show up but I'd be gone.

"Eight, seven, six . . ."

Okay, okay, I gave in. *Okay.*

I had to try it, I didn't have a choice: 06-13-00.

Immediately, the countdown stopped. The beeping stopped. The cabinet drawer clicked open. June 13, the year 2000. It was Eva-Kate's birthday.

What the fuck, Mom? My whole face felt heavy, like it could melt off into a puddle at my feet. What did it mean? Why did she . . . why would she . . .

I'd have to get to that later.

Inside the file cabinet was exactly what I'd hoped for: patient files arranged alphabetically. I flipped to the *K* section and pulled out Eva-Kate's, then took the thick stack of papers and spread them out across the couch. Some were loose-leaf papers, others were entire notebooks. My mom had written volumes on Eva-Kate. The first notebook dated back to 2009, when Eva-Kate was only nine years old. I would have been eight that year, the year I met Rachel Ames. I couldn't wrap my mind around this. The idea—that Eva-Kate Kelly had been coming to see my mom since I was eight years old, that she spent countless hours in my own backyard for eight or nine years while I was in the house less than twenty feet away, not having a clue—was disorienting and slippery. As I tried to make sense of it all, the facts slipped out of my reach like little fish.

"Okay, okay," I said, taking a deep breath and opening the notebook to the first page. It read:

Evelyn Kathleen
March 1, 2009

— Nine years old, has been acting since the age of four, has starred in a successful sitcom since the age of seven. Understandably more stressed than the average nine-year-old.

— She's the family breadwinner. Feels the pressure of her mom and sister (twin, identical) relying on her for money. Dad left before she was born. Says she "knows for a fact" that neither of her parents love her. Believes her mom actually hates her.

— Mom is an ex beauty queen who ran away
  from home at an early age. Debbie McKelvoy.
  Had dreams of becoming a movie star but
  stopped pursuing it when she gave birth to
  Eva-Kate and her sister, Liza-Jane. Classic
  situation of a stage mother driven by a
  hope—conscious or subconscious—to live
  vicariously through her children.

— EK says Debbie is verbally abusive to her, but
  not to LJ. Has been telling EK that she's a
  "bad apple" for as long as she can remember.
  Tells her that she was "born with dead eyes"
  and that she has "has her father's evil in her."
  As a result of these beliefs, Debbie has refused
  to show affection of any kind for EK,
  reserving it all for LJ, who she believes to be
  the "good" child.

— "My mom's one of those people who believes
  in good and evil."

— Debbie insisted on taking EK to therapy to
  get rid of the "evil" that she "inherited" from
  her father. Puts EK alone in a taxi from
  Burbank to get here, which EK says she is
  completely comfortable with.

— No matter how much money EK makes
for the family, her mom won't stop
persecuting her with punishments. When
asked, EK refused to elaborate on said
punishments.

— Wonders if her mom is projecting onto her or
if she truly was born wicked.

— Used the word "projecting" in this context
three different times. For a nine-year-old, her
vocabulary is advanced, almost eerily so. An
acutely precocious child.

Evelyn Kathleen
March 8, 2009

— EK showed up smelling like cigarettes.

— Very gloomy today. Stared off for most of the
session.

— Dreamed her house crumbled around them,
and then mom and LJ turned to stone and
crumbled too. Recurring dream. Sometimes
it's mom and LJ, sometimes it's her costars,

sometimes her agent. Randy Kessler-Stevens. Mentioned that one time it was a man named Dr. Silver. Reminder: look up Randy and Dr. Silver.

— "I know it doesn't sound that scary, but when it's happening it's like the worst feeling in the world."

— Crumbling house represents . . . ?

— EK having a hard time concentrating during lessons, which she takes on set. Feels that it's not fair to expect her to work and go to school and be good at both.

— Envies LJ's "real" life.

— "All she does is sit around reading books and everyone loves her."

— When asked if she loves her sister, EK said, "We used to love each other, but not anymore."

I scoured the first year of notes, searching for pertinent details, transfixed by every word. Here and there I found new insights into Eva-Kate's subconscious, but it wasn't enough. None of it added up to the explanation I was looking for. Notes from 2010 showed themes of rebellion and taking back power. Here I learned that Eva-Kate's mom had been making her pay for her own therapy. It seemed with my mom's help she decided she'd keep paying for therapy but not for the rest of Debbie's and Liza's expenses. My mom had suggested the possibility of Eva-Kate becoming an emancipated minor. She'd encouraged Eva-Kate to hire a lawyer, but Eva-Kate had rejected the idea, saying Debbie would kill her for it. This was the year she met her first friend, Ruby Jones. They'd met at a strange party their parents had dragged them to, where they'd been the only kids, and spent the evening outside behind a tree brainstorming a plan to run away from home.

By the time I'd finished that second year, the clock read 1:00 A.M. Almost three hours had passed since I'd started reading. I had a dozen missed calls from Eva-Kate and twice that many from my mom. I turned my phone off and threw it across the room. I hated them both.

In 2011, Rob entered the picture. Just a new costar, two years older, who irritated her by using incorrect grammar and making fun of her pink Converse high-tops. She knew his grammar was off because she'd started paying attention during class. Learning made her feel in control, like she held some amount of power over the people around her, who were "simpletons" and "imbeciles" and "cretins."

In 2012, she spoke more and more about "realness" and feeling fake. My mom noted hickeys on her neck and increasingly nervous energy. She wore less clothing and more makeup, she got invited to parties in Hollywood and went to them just because her mom hated it. Then she started going to them for the drugs and a boy she obsessed over but wouldn't name, and the things they'd do together that my mom wrote about in her notes using only euphemisms. She was only twelve. One day during her session she broke down sobbing, saying that her mom was right, she was born without a soul. She said the tabloids and blogs all called her Barbie Girl and speculated about the realness of her breasts, which made her want to kill someone. Or herself.

I felt my eyelids getting heavy and checked the clock. Another two hours had passed. Princess Leia scratched at the door, but I knew I couldn't let her out, she'd have to wait. I counted and realized I hadn't slept since the first night at the Madonna Inn, but I had to keep reading. My mom would be home in the morning and I didn't trust her to tell me the truth.

The notes from 2013 were just four or five pages paper-clipped together. I took the clip off and a page from the middle fell to the floor. I reached down to pick it up, and in the dreary, algae-green light I came face-to-face with my own name. *Finally.*

Evelyn Kathleen
May 5, 2013

— EK noticed the picture of Justine in the back
of the office. Didn't know I had a daughter and
looked hurt to find out.

— Discussed transference, the redirection of
childhood emotions onto a therapist. EK
agreed that in this case, the feelings are
abandonment and radical inferiority, but
wasn't reassured. Said she was fine, but
appeared agitated for the rest of the
session.

— Asked if I cared about my daughter more than
I cared about her. Reminder: Must discuss
next time.

Evelyn Kathleen
May 19, 2013

— EK asked about Justine again. Wanted to
know about her personality and her interests.
I reminded her that this time is for us to
discuss her, not me or my family.

— Continued to speculate throughout session what sort of person Justine might be.

— Was determined to get a response and became frustrated when I wouldn't give it to her.

— Eventually backed down when asked about boyfriend. Attention switched fully off Justine and onto boyfriend like a light switch had been flipped.

— For twenty minutes discussed constant competition between them.

— Thinks the fans like him a lot more than they like her ever since his album came out. Worries they'll turn into "Justin and Britney," meaning that he'll break up with her and go on to be internationally glorified, while she's labeled crazy and eventually discarded.

— Exploring the concept of "future tripping" seemingly had no effect.

— Dreamed the set of <u>Jennie and Jenny</u> was crumbling around her and she was alone. Then she turned to stone and crumbled too.

Evelyn Kathleen

January 4, 2014

— EK mentioned Justine for the first time since
May of 2013.

— Proudly informed me that she'd found
Justine's Instagram and could tell that she
was a really "down-to-earth girl" and "the
perfect daughter." "Wholesome." We
revisited the projection of perfection onto
somebody, and that nobody actually is
perfect.

— Acted as if she didn't hear me.

— Said her boyfriend talks about "real, down-to-
earth girls," and that he'd probably love
Justine. She thinks he's secretly in love with
LJ and that's why.

— Fixating on the dichotomies of good/bad and
real/fake and how they pertain to herself and
LJ. Doesn't seem to realize this was an
arbitrary assignment by a mentally unwell
mother, not the truth. Although I do worry
about self-fulfilling prophecies. Thinks if she

were real and good then she could be loved,
but couldn't describe what either word meant
to her.

— Lingered on the photograph of Justine as she
left. It shouldn't have been out there in the
first place. I moved it to the back part of the
room where it belonged.

In a twilight daze, I flipped to the next page and saw
that it was dated August of 2015, over a year after the
previous notes. It occurred to me that this set of papers
wasn't clipped together based on chronological order,
but instead by a unifying theme: me.

From there on out I scanned through, looking only
for my name. This is what I found:

Evelyn Kathleen
August 22, 2015

— EK says she knows from Instagram that
Justine is at Bellflower. Didn't think J would
have posted that sort of thing, but Eva-Kate
showed me the image in question. Of a
gate covered in ivy. When I asked
what made her think she knew the name
of the building, she explained how she'd

used geo-tagging to determine the location and looked it up from there. A major point of concern.

— Reported that she'd done her research and learned that Bellflower is a "mental hospital." Wanted to know what she'd done to get sent away, but accepted that I wouldn't go into it with her.

— Renewed fixation with Justine has become alarming.

— "I'm sorry if I'm being inappropriate. I'm just curious. I wonder what happens to a real girl when she loses touch with reality."

Evelyn Kathleen
December 12, 2015

— EK seemed sedated and dreamy, perhaps on pills.

— Bright blue tongue and teeth, which she attributed to candy.

— Made no effort to get rid of the blue.

— Asked if it was Justine she saw down the street walking a white fluffy dog. Quickly followed the question with another one: Had I ever mentioned her to Justine?

— Explained the importance of patient-client confidentiality, which seemed to please her.

— Asked how Justine was doing since she came home from Bellflower.

— Becoming harder and harder to divert the conversation away from Justine.

Evelyn Kathleen
April 30, 2018

— EK making incredible progress. High spirits throughout session.

— Hasn't had nightmares in months.

— Shaking off rumors about boyfriend and LJ with impressive maturity.

— Hasn't mentioned Justine in almost a year. Greatly reassuring.

— A weight seems to have been lifted ever since a judge granted her emancipation. Working with a realtor to find her own home, far away from her mom and LJ.

— Still agitated when talking about the friendship between boyfriend and LJ. Slips easily into a paranoid headspace.

— Very accepting of my upcoming trip. Looking forward to a month of independence, but adamant about starting back up upon my return.

— Did end up mentioning Justine, but only to ask if she was coming with me.

When I finished reading, a savage exhale escaped my mouth. I'd been holding my breath for God knows how long. *She knew about my mom's summer trip two months before I did. Did she know about the divorce before I did too?*

I didn't need to read any more, I just needed to get myself far away. The hair on my arms stood on end from knowing Eva-Kate was so nearby and that my mom would be home within hours. Where would I go? I couldn't go to my dad, or Aunt Jillian, both of whom I'd avoided like the plague the last few weeks. I couldn't go to Riley, who I'd ghosted and who'd accused me of sociopathy. I paced the room to help me think, chewing on the tips of my silvery-blue hair. And thank God for that color, because it reminded me of something I'd forgotten since the shock of hearing my mom's voice on Eva-Kate's answering machine: I had ten thousand dollars in my bank account.

I looked up the Ace Hotel in downtown Los Angeles and booked the most expensive room they had: a luxury loft for five hundred dollars a night. I figured I'd start with six nights and go from there. I wish I'd known then that I'd only be needing two.

CHAPTER 24

SO HELP ME GOD

I can swear that what I'm about to write is the solemn truth, whether you believe it or not.

Leaving home, I didn't have enough time to get into my room and pack a bag—plus, Eva-Kate might have been able to see me through my window from across the canal—so I put my mom's notes back as I had found them, clipped the leash in my purse onto Princess Leia, ordered an Uber, then stepped on my phone and smashed it to pieces. Then I was gone.

In the Ace Hotel lobby, they made it very clear to me that minors couldn't check in without a guardian, so I took cash out from the ATM and handed them a grand in hundred-dollar bills. The night I'd met Eva-Kate, I hadn't been DGAF. Now I was.

My room was on the eleventh floor and half the size of my whole house. I had a view of the entire city, which at nighttime was just a sea of glittery, pulsing light. How pretty it looked from such great heights. *Come down now, they'll say.* I turned up the radio and opened a bottle of Johnnie Walker from the mini fridge. I considered taking a shower in the minimalistically posh bathroom, but when the king-sized bed caught my eye I wanted so badly to be in it. I made sure to take my meds before I forgot, then took Princess Leia and got under the blanket, which had that expensive combination of simultaneous weight and weightlessness. The clock on the bedside table was a retro-style flip clock in a sleek wooden case. It showed the day and date as well as the time. I stared at it, mesmerized by the quiet flutter of one moment slipping into the next, and in minutes, maybe even seconds, I was asleep.

✳ ✳ ✳

I woke up to a thunderous banging against my door. For a moment I had no idea where I was or how I'd gotten there, but when I looked around in disoriented panic, heart racing, I saw it was my hotel room, and the clock by my bedside read: WEDNESDAY 8:13 A.M. *That's not possible*, I thought, *nobody can sleep through a whole day.*

The door shook again, this time so hard I could see the brass chain bolt getting ready to pop open.

"LAPD, open up!"

Holy fuck, I whispered to myself. *What the hell happened?*

"One minute!" I called out, bombarded by thoughts of everything that could have gone wrong. "I'll be right there!"

I hurried to the door and struggled to steady my hands as I fidgeted with the chain bolt. When I finally got it off the hook, the cops pushed the door open, sending me stumbling backward. Two policemen stood before me, one burly and tan, the other a little bit older with a graying goatee and receding hairline.

"Justine Childs?" the burly one asked.

"Yes?" My chest tightened. The two men loomed over me, their stiff uniforms marking them unmistakably as the couriers of bad news.

"We're going to have to take you down to the station for questioning. You'll need a guardian present. Is there someone you can call?"

I stared, blinking dumbly, the word *guardian* undulating like a jellyfish in my mind.

"Miss Childs?" the older one asked.

"Oh, um, sorry. Yes. But . . . can I . . . can I ask . . . what this is about?"

"It's about Eva-Kate Kelly," the burly one explained, cold and blunt. "We believe you were close?"

"*Eva-Kate? Is she okay?*" I asked, though I knew the answer. If she were okay, they wouldn't be standing here.

"No, Miss Childs," he said, clearing his throat. "She's dead."

CHAPTER 25

HUMAN AFTER ALL

*T*hey found her body floating in the canal with a fatal knife wound on her left side, just below her rib cage. I thought it would take a lot more to kill a force like Eva-Kate Kelly, but it turned out she was only human after all.

I thought her death would be the end, but in so many ways it was only the beginning. My Instagram following went up to the millions: 1.4 million, then 4 million, then 11. I couldn't go outside without facing the dazzling assault of paparazzi flashbulbs. They lit the canal from across the bridge day and night.

My mom was home and I was trapped there with her. She refused to let me outside and said it was for my own good. Twice, while she was asleep, I was able to get out and have a cigarette in the alley behind the house. The cameras caught me both times, a ghost-white deer in the headlights, startled stiff. Later they'd call me cold, they'd wonder if I was heartless, they'd say I didn't look sad enough about Eva-Kate's death, they'd say I looked numb, like a girl who didn't care.

But listen carefully when I tell you that, despite what you'll hear, those first days after Eva-Kate's death were the scariest of my life. The room they questioned me in was cold and lit by panels of overhead fluorescents that flickered off and on, buzzing, snapping, flooding the room with acid-white light I thought I'd drown in. I swiveled wildly between denial and despair. The memory of her haunted me—her soft lips and sharp tongue, her grace and indecency, her affectation and desperation. The memory of her was still so alive that sometimes I thought I could reach out and wrap my arms around it. But she was gone, and I was free-falling.

I forgave her for lying to me and I minimized the lie. I made it romantic in my mind. I spent my time wondering what we could have become, wondering about the deep trove of information I'd found in my mom's office, wondering when I'd confront her about it, wondering what Taylor Swift would do right now if she were me. #WhatWouldTaylorSwiftDo? #WWTSD?

She'd write about it, that's what she'd do.

And I knew that was what I had to do if I wanted to

keep my head above water. If I wanted to stay sane, I'd have to get it all on paper, where it couldn't swallow me up.

If I wanted to stay sane, I was going to have to tell the story, and if I was going to tell the story, I would have to start at the beginning, and so I began:

Eva-Kate Kelly.

Is this story really about a person with three first names? Could anything be more tedious than a person with three first names? I know you, I can imagine you rolling your eyes thinking you're too good for a girl with three first names, let alone an entire story about a girl with three first names, but the truth is most likely that no matter who you are and no matter how hard you're capable of rolling your eyes, Eva-Kate Kelly would love that you think you're too good for her and her three first names, she would revel in the few short moments it took her to prove you wrong, she would chew you up and she would spit you out, she would impale you with the fire-green lasers that were her eyes, stare into you and then through you, so that you'd wonder if you ever existed at all. It would take you months to recover and you'd never really be the same again. That was the Eva-Kate I first came to know, anyway.

ACKNOWLEDGMENTS

This book would not have been possible without help from my family, friends, and incredible support team.

Thank you to my parents, Caron and Mark, for encouraging me to live a creative life and supporting me in my writing dreams. For the record, they are (almost) nothing like the parents in the novel you just read. Thank you to my sister, Natasha, for believing in me and for being the official style and home decor consultant on this project.

Thank you to my editor, Kate Farrell, for understanding this story even better than I do, my agent Richard Abate, who has been an advocate of this book from day one, and Melissa de la Cruz, whose magic touch brought it all to life.

The following people have been by my side on the

journey of writing my first novel, and for that I am eternally grateful: Jenny Bailey, Hannah Denyer, Omar Doom, Quinn Falconer, Brad Kaiserman, Kasey Koop, Kathleen Koster, Liana Maeby, Amanda Montell, B. J. Novak, Cindy Post, Emily Robinson, Sophia Rossi, Arpy Sarkissian, Ali Segel, Kellen Solano, Cameron Solano, Scarlett Solano, Robert Wieder, and a very special thank you to Jason Solano, who was with me in the trenches from beginning to end.

Thank you to Abby Frucht, Ellen Lesser, Francesca Lia Block, Sarah Maclay, Clint McCown, and Domenic Stansberry for their guidance and inspiration.

Lastly, thank you to my grandma Ellie and nana Doreen, who this book is dedicated to because of the nature of their belief in me, which was unconditional and life-changing.

Fake Plastic World

THE SEQUEL TO
Fake Plastic Girl—
MARCH 2020